WHEN YOU FIND OUT WHAT YOU'RE MADE OF

MICHELLE VON ESCHEN

Dedicated to those in pieces.

TABLE OF CONTENTS

WHEN YOU FIND OUT
WHAT YOU'RE MADE OF

MICHELLE VON ESCHEN

WHEN YOU FIND OUT WHAT YOU'RE MADE OF

Tape recorder clicks on.

Dr. Heston with patient Natali Costa.
Begin Session.

Your mother mentioned you had a yard sale?

Yeah, I could see the looks they were giving me, even through my midnight tinted sunglasses, even from within the cool shadows of the oversized umbrella I sat beneath.

It was a fair enough day for a yard sale. The multi-colored falling leaves announced autumn, but the occasional sun breaks still clung to the idea of summer. The strangers picked through my things, their deal-seeking hands dug through box after box, scrutinizing every item for value as, in between finds, they scrutinized me."

Why do you think they were paying special attention to you?

I don't know. Maybe because I was selling so many nice things?

Tell me about the items at this sale.

I can tell you about the weirdos who showed up.

A man emerged from the fucking chaos of my driveway clutching his claim. 'Is there anything wrong with this?' He asked me as he held up my tower heater in a way reminiscent of a nurse presenting a baby. Nothing wrong with it at all, ten fingers and toes, I wanted to say.

Instead I told him it was in perfect *condition*, but I laughed afterward because the unit also offered a cooling option. I don't think the dude heard the subtle stress I put on the word 'condition', or maybe he wasn't aware of all the tower's capabilities. The thing had a giant red and blue sticker on it so I thought it was kinda obvious.

Then he asked me if there was an outlet nearby where he could plug it in to test it, but I assured him it would operate at peak performance because I had used it for a brutal year of insane seasonal adherence. That boiling summer and freezing winter, I'm sure the little tower was the only thing that kept me alive.

Why would you get rid of something so useful?

It absolutely terrifies me now.

Can you expand on that? Why are you afraid of the space heater?

Next thing I know, this guy has a chubby thumb shoved in my face, a white sticker stuck to its tip. 'The price is too low,' he said as I pretended to read the price on the tag. I already knew what it said, I mean, I wrote it myself. I told him it was a deal, priced to sell, yadda yadda. Then I let him know that the tower heater rotates too. I moved my hand side to side to mimic the oscillation. Made me feel like a used car salesman, you know, when they point out the cup holders in a minivan or maybe a flight attendant gesturing to emergency exits.

Apparently that was the wrong thing to say because then it was 'definitely underpriced' according to him. Dude had the audacity to say he didn't trust me and then said he'd take it off my hands for two bucks less than I'd priced it!

We'll come back to the space heater. What else did you sell?

Oh, and then the next lady was a real nut. A stay-at-home-mom type who'd probably dropped the kids off at school and then hunted the city for yard sales to get her savings fix. I could tell by her outfit that she shopped at thrift stores too. She wore a faded "I climbed the Astoria Column" sweater atop her two-sizes-too-big dad jeans, rolled up to expose her mismatched socks. One was covered in cats, the other, watermelons.

She had this woven basket in her hands and I have no idea where she found it, but it wasn't mine. Maybe something she scored from another yard market? I couldn't focus on what was in it yet because her hands caught my eye. They were covered in papercuts, dried glue, and construction paper confetti. Oh joy, she was a crafter too! Maybe even a couponer. She was the epitome of the deal-chaser. Deep discounts were the tornado she searched for endlessly. She was a child-rearing, craft-making maniac. I could tell she'd found something wonderful in my things for her face was aglow with an ecstasy normally attributed to drugs of some kind.

What made her so happy?

My mom, you know how she is. She's a decorator. She's always making things look nice, or ruining them by adding too much glam, or bling, or some other shiny shit. Over the years, her thing has been to gift me candles and things to hold them. She always picks the super smelly ones too. Well, this lady in my yard, she found that pile of candles and candle accessories and she wanted them all.

'These are high quality candles,' she told me. I didn't know there was such a thing, but I nodded my head because that seemed like a better idea than asking her to explain something I didn't care about.

How would your mother feel if she knew you'd sold all the candles she'd gifted you?

The couponer lady started to tell me all the awesome things she could make by melting them. I didn't want to hear any of it, frankly it was making me anxious, so I told her she could just take them. So technically I didn't sell my mom's candles. I could even retell it to sound like a craft crazy lady ran off with them if I need to. They didn't work how I wanted them too anyway.

We've talked about making things up before. You

shouldn't start down that road. How could candles not work?

It was the woman who bought all my blankets that nearly pushed me over the edge. She kept glancing around like she didn't want to be seen in my neighborhood. She wore sunglasses darker than mine, so oversized on her face she looked alien. Kinda deathly thin like one too.

This bitch thought someone had died. She asked me if the 'estate owner' had made the quilts herself. I lied to her, I did. I said yes, but I got them all on clearance at Target or some place. I kinda hoped she'd take them home and brag to her rich friends about the history of them. Then in that way, I made her a liar. That's what she gets for not taking her sunglasses off to talk to me and for being all judgy and ashamed about my neighborhood.

Did you take yours off to speak with her?

No, but that's not the point. It was *my* yard sale.

You seem to notice many details about other people. If they were staring at you as much as you said they were, what might they see?

Are you asking me to describe myself, doc?

Sure, if that's how you interpret the question.

I hate when you pull that therapist shit. I don't know. I'm changing.

That's something I'd like to talk about next. Your mother said you've lost a lot of weight recently and

that you aren't keeping much food in your house?

Things were fine until she showed up at my place unannounced and uninvited. She let herself in with the key she insists on keeping. 'You're too thin' were the first words across her botox-bloated lips as she walked in the door, followed by 'you aren't eating enough.' A funny thing for my stickbug mother to mention. She's anorexic you know and doesn't give a fuck that it'll probably kill her. She cares about the way her gold bangles hang on her dainty wrists, the straightness of the legs of her designer jeans, and that every time her friends come around they compliment on her amazing ability to stay thin while living a chaotic life as the owner of a cutting edge New York art gallery.

I can't believe I came out of that woman. If you want to help someone, doc, maybe you should talk to her.

What about the appointments with friends you've been missing?

I think I've missed a couple hot yoga classes and a ramen date. That's hardly anything to be concerned about. Are you my appointment keeper now?

Your mother, and myself too honestly, are worried because these behaviors--the selling or giving away of belongings, the lack of appetite, the shutting out of loved ones-- they are symptomatic of depression, of potential suicide.

Ha! My mom thinks I'm gonna off myself? Do you know how many times she's had her stomach pumped to bring her back from death? That woman eats pills like candy. I'm not gonna kill myself, okay. But I really don't know what's gonna happen to me. I have to be so careful now. All it would take is one mistake for things to go horribly wrong.

Is that what happened with your arms? I can see the bandages. Is this something you did to yourself?

I wasn't trying to hurt myself, okay. I was doing some work. Trying to mend things. I've been handling the change as best I can, okay?

You sound scared. What fears do you have? Can we revisit the space heater now?

My mom should be happy that I'm saving on the electricity bill. I don't even turn on the heat anymore.

I didn't want to tell anyone this, but I'm here and you've brought me right up to it. Maybe you have some ideas about what is happening. You know the feeling, doc, when your finger finds something on your body it didn't expect to come across?

Yes, I do.

Like a wound turned scab in pursuit of healing, a raised mole so tall and squishy it could be a mushroom for all you fucking know. A bump that's most definitely cancer, but more likely, you've had it since you were born. Or when your tongue discovers the canker sore on the inside of your cheek and proceeds to mess with it until you've convinced yourself it'll never disappear in such a wet and hostile environment. In fact, when did you ever *not* have that canker sore, right?

Well, I must have noticed before, how could I miss the soft patch at the base of my skull, just below my hairline? But as I found it during an intense shampooing, it felt new, foreign, *strange*. I fiddled with the tender skin, the surface anomaly begged me to touch it to the point of irritation. I couldn't keep my pointer finger from prodding. It wasn't until the digit felt constricted that I realized it had sunk in up to its middle knuckle, buried in my flesh, enveloped like a pig in a blanket.

It took some tugging to remove it and because the water ran over me, the finger came out with a moist, suctioning sound. I toweled off with a tenderness reserved for infants or the infirm and achieved amazing feats of contortion between the large bathroom mirror and the smaller one on the door of the medicine cabinet in order to examine with my eyes the sinkhole. I'm still impressed with the calm I maintained as I stared into that abyss on the back of my neck. I should have been freaking out, right? I should have called a doctor. But I felt no pain, which was surprising, seeing as how my body should have been squirting spinal fluid or something from the depths.

I turned down the thermostat that night, terrified I'd melt in my sleep. I imagined myself stuck to the quilt, melding with the fabric, oozing into the threading, and discoloring the patchwork with my oiliness. It, my tissue paper to the doughnut I had become. I didn't even know then if I needed sleep still.

In bed, I decided to have the yard sale. Get rid of everything that might melt me.

Am I right, Natali, in assessing that you believe you are made out of wax?

How else can you explain the hole in my neck? The lack of pain and appetite? The sensitivity to heat?

Can you show me the hole?

No, I filled it back in. And I'm not showing you my arms either so don't ask. You just scribbled something down. Are we coming back to this topic later?

The candles, the blankets and space heater make sense. But why did you get rid of your cat?

I knew it, moving on so quickly. I got rid of Bianca because she was causing problems. I took her to the animal shelter, told the overly friendly, scrubs-garbed crew a lie about income or moving or something to answer their nosy questions as to why she couldn't live with me anymore. How could I explain that she was a menace simply because she was a cat? Her claws, no matter how trimmed, were leaving tiny, circular impressions as she kneaded her paws into my dough body. It was too much work to pinch and reshape the surface, like refilling a few dozen nail holes in the walls of an empty apartment to get the security deposit back. Tedious, a pain. She was making a war-torn country of my outer layer with her tiny razor blades.

And the food?

The truth is that I haven't been eating at all. I sip water and room temperature tea. Where would the food go in my wax stomach? Would it sit there like a compost pile, steaming and decomposing over time. At least, I think, the water will run over and around any internal mounds. I can just feel the lumps inside of me.

What are your plans for this new future?

At a point, I'll become immobile. My mother, the art gallery owner, the curator, will move me to a wax museum to be with the others.

The others?

Those who have turned. The people who, like me, started out alive, but made this transition into something else after they found out what they were made of.

End Session.

WILDFLOWER

I yearn for those fall days. He'd come in from playing soccer and I'd help peel off his muddy jersey. I remember that fresh and exhausted look. His bright eyes, those rosy cheeks set atop the Pacific Northwest shade of ghost that was the usual color of his skin. I recall him needing things, as children do, and how often I could come through for him. He was ten. I was still one of his heroes.

Day 1

The rash came suddenly, as quickly as the leaves on the tree across the street changed from deep fern to brilliant lemon. He already took his own baths, sometimes showers, but I was still the designated muddy shirt "peeler offer," as he called me and filling that need, well, that's when I noticed the marks.

They spread from his spine and were individually irregular in shape, though nearly rorschach in symmetry from his left to right side. For now they were scarlet, and in glaring contrast to the pasty white of his skin.

I did the usual motherly interrogation, does it hurt, itch, when did it start? He responded with a quick shrug- a perfect ten-year-oldism -part I don't know, part I don't care. I blamed it on the field he kicked ball in, the water, the humid Seattle air. Then, I blamed it on the anti-vaxxers, just for good measure. Fault lied somewhere.

On the first day, he wasn't bothered, nor was he in pain. So I didn't do a damn thing.

Day 2

My sleep was nightmare-ridden. They were the same bad dreams I had when he was an infant. In them, I am terrified to bathe my son, fearful the baby smell will wash away. Forever replaced by the Dove or Ivory or whatever soap had been on sale the last shopping trip. I have anxiety over his teenage years to come, when he'll grow like a weed and hormones will take over to replace that youthful scent with the heavy odor of sweat. And then when he grows self-conscious of that, some spray-on musk of his choosing. And he'll become someone I don't know, a human I cannot recognize. What a difficult thing, for a woman to watch her boy become a man. And now all I wanted to do was bathe him, scrub the bad off with love and elbow grease. He wouldn't allow it these days, defiant to the point of screaming. The rash didn't change the fact that he was "too old" for his mom to see him "all the way naked". I just wanted to make sure I got to see him grow up.

The neighborhood appeared peaceful that day. I shook off the unease of my dreams by noon and he and I practiced our Sunday afternoon rituals of lazing around the house and snacking too much. I washed his bedding in allergen-free soap with water so hot it would kill anything that might be causing the trouble.

I remember sitting behind him, me on the couch and he on the floor, while he clobbered baddies in one of his video games. I had a view of the back of his head, which he still moved directionally with the turns of the game. He needed a haircut-another struggle between us.

"Mom, did you see that?" He asked me several times over the course of the afternoon after some particularly spectacular boss battles. I praised him, but honestly I hadn't seen any of the game. I was too busy watching him squirm in his skin.

Day 3

After a night of scratching to the point of bleeding, he missed his first day of school. Overnight, the rash spread to more of his body than I could reasonably cover. The crimson patches peeked below his preferred gym shorts, and wrapped red and raw around his neck at the collar line.

Standing at the living room window, I noticed the streets and yards were dotted with the other children of the neighborhood and their skin was just as blotchy and red as my son's. I called the other parents from the soccer team. Most didn't answer, those who did confirmed their children had the same rash and that the doctors could do nothing for it. A few mentioned something bigger, something global, but I tuned it out. Only my son mattered. The child in front of me wearing winter gloves so he didn't destroy himself like a fussy infant with long nails and no self-awareness.

Helpless is an understatement. I, an ant watching

a tsunami roll in, swept up before I knew it, powerless against a force much greater than myself. It was my duty to protect my progeny, but no salve or rub stopped the welts from growing, changing. I ran him bath after bath, which he allowed on the third day. I dug out the heating pads and ice packs, googled home remedies and ancient treatments and hoodoo witch magic. I prayed to God, who hadn't heard from me in a long time. And not surprisingly, he never replied. The rash darkened to merlots and plums. He looked like an abuse case, covered from head to toe in bruising. The color change mislead me. I glimpsed hope of healing. I was wrong.

"It hurts now, mommy," he said to me as I closed the book we'd been reading before bed for a week. I hadn't been "mommy" since his sixth birthday. That tender word and the layer of whine it swam in betrayed his suffering.

Day 4

His crying woke me that morning. It came in brittle waves, breaking on the shore of his parched throat. And even though the other parents said it would be a wasted trip, I loaded him up and off to the doctor. Born too small and constantly sick as a toddler, we spent so much time in hospitals that I grew to loathe them or anything close to them. The smells, the fake calm when worlds were ending in every other room, the cafeteria food. They rarely seem to know what's happening with someone, and when they do, it's never good news.

He echoed what the parents had told me: "you

won't see an improvement" and "there's no known cure." He called the rash "exotic" and berated me for allowing days to pass before seeking help. But how would seeing him any sooner have helped when there wasn't a thing to be done? That's when I allowed myself to watch the news, another thing I'd been avoiding. There were parents marching, demanding answers and a cure. I wanted to join them, but I couldn't understand how they'd managed to leave their poor, suffering children alone.

I picked up words through my tears: pandemic, world-wide, affecting prepubescent children, including babies in utero. Nature was angry and asking for reprieve. *Enough*, it bellowed. *Enough of you things!* We'd tipped the scale too much. I didn't blame her. We deserved something drastic, but talk about a low blow. The earth fought back with a vengeance to maintain the balance. I'd seen a movie like that once. A lot of people died. But why all the children?

It might have been a comfort, to know that so many others were experiencing the same thing, but it could do nothing for his pain. They instructed us to isolate those exhibiting symptoms. Instead, I held him in my lap, as much as I still could hold his nearly preteen body and I held him as close as possible. He writhed as I cradled him, as restless as his newborn self had been. I put SpongeBob on, telling myself it would help to calm him, but my own eyes needed distraction from the tiny lines, new veins of some kind that were inching along their way beneath his skin. Whatever it was, it wasn't superficial. It was inside him too. I ran my fingers through his hair, which had begun to change texture. No longer soft, but coarse and dry, like reed grass. I almost enjoyed the rustling sound it made as I soothed him, until I realized it broke off in pieces between my fingers.

Day 5

He stopped talking last night and I can't convince him to leave his bed. I've built an army of stuffed animals to keep him company and a cocoon of blankets to hold him. He won't put any clothes on, as the slightest pressure on his skin causes excruciating pain. I can see all colors of something alien beneath the thin surface, pushing up for light. My son is a Jackson Pollock painting laid flat and cut to resemble a human child.

I've made camp on his floor and done some work in surrounding myself with comforts as well. I spread his baby pictures out before me, drank a cup of the most calming tea I could find in my cupboards, and wrapped myself in a quilt made during my pregnancy. When they're born, it seems as though you'll have them forever. Their vibrancy, born of youth and naivety, boosts your own sense of well-being. You feel invincible together.

I read to him, over our blanket mountains. When he began snoring, I believe that is the last time I heard any remnant of his voice. I'm writing this down in hopes of looking back on it someday as a thing we survived together. Like chickenpox, puberty, or his first day. But he hasn't had any of those things yet and I don't know that he will. Children shouldn't die before their parents.

Day 6

He'll take water and nothing else. He looks like a scarecrow in his skin, bits of straw or something like it, poking out of fissures near his wrists, his body lumpy from poorly distributed stuffing. Like someone dug a hole and then refilled it, the dirt not fitting in quite the same as before. A suggestion of a boy, but nowhere near the real thing. His smell is gone, replaced by an earthy, heavy scent, like the air here after rain. I can no longer lie to myself. No longer tell myself he is going to pull through. My tough little boy, my premie who fought hard and made it out of NICU, my only child, my only anything. These would be his final days.

I'm ashamed to admit that I left him alone for hours today. I can't stop crying and it doesn't seem right to add to his suffering. Instead I'm keeping my wine rack company, choking down the reds, appreciating our combined bitterness. An evening with peace of mind, on the floor of my kitchen, which is spinning while in the other room, my world was ending.

His pulse is weak as I read to him before bed. Even if he is listening, I'm slurring my words so much the book must sound foreign. I place the bookmark lovingly into the pages, a flower at a grave I could visit someday. I hold his hand, but he doesn't hold mine back. Moments like this, you try not to take them personally. I remind myself it's because he's ill, and not because he's growing up. He won't be growing up. God, I need him to grow up!

I make it to my room before the sobbing explodes from me and bury my head in my pillows to stifle the noise.

Day 7

As soon as I wake, I know he is gone. We are dissected. The house hasn't felt this empty since before his birth, when his father left. Like the still bathwater of a suicide, you just know there's no way for life to exist in such quiet. I can't bear to see his body yet, so I walk closely to the wall opposite his bedroom door, with my head down, straight to the kitchen to brew coffee I won't drink.

My thoughts, like my stomach, are reeling. And though my head isn't pounding yet, I know the hangover will find me. It'll do mighty work on my broken self when it does. I watch the tendrils of steam climb the air like vines, grasping for something invisible, and even that seems insulting. How can nature steal the only love left in my life? My baby, grown from a minute seed inside my body, slowly taken over by something of his own biology. I'll reach for the nothing of him for the rest of my days. His room, a shrine. Untouched for years. A holy place.

I set the full mug down a touch to hard in the sink and it shatters. How appropriate. Pieces like everything else. I gather the shards and the courage to say goodbye, push myself away from the coffee, and the table, and the kitchen, and walk the hall back to his room. The doorknob is cool beneath my hand. I hold it for some time, as though if the door stayed shut there'd be possibility he is still alive. Schrödinger's Child. But I can smell nature and as I open the door, the scent of detritus is overwhelming. Pollen floats in the air.

A bed of beautiful flowers has birthed from his

body. Petals in shades of colors I've never seen before. I lay in them, unconcerned if I might be next to bloom. His field envelops me and for a moment I feel closer to him than I ever have before. It is then, when my heart stops pounding so loudly in my chest, that I hear the wails of the others around the neighborhood, waking to find their young ones gone.

SIDE EFFECTS

"Do you need a larger chair?" the judge asks a man who resembles a monster both in size and grimace, whose weight is pushing screams out of the frail, stackable seat that has disappeared beneath his bulk. "Do we have a larger chair?" The judge asks the security guard positioned near the front of the courtroom. The metal legs are bending, the judge is certain. "Can someone find a bigger chair?" He doesn't want to anger the man in the dissolving seat. "Should we have him stand instead of sit?" Each time he asks a chair-related question, the panic in his voice escalates. It's as though finding a chair or a solution to the chair issue is more important than determining what the beast of a man has done. Someone finds a bench and drags it in front of the testimonial stand. The giant, his muscles threatening the seams of his orange jumpsuit, pulls himself off the dying chair, which lets out a humanlike sigh of relief as he lumbers around to the long wooden pew. Reinforced with love from a nail gun, it's only slightly more inclined to support his form. He hunches with hands handcuffed at the wrists, steel creaking like an old trestle against the weight and power of a heavier load, clasped in his lap. His feet are crossed one over the other. An oversized, underskilled, unconfident child looking as though he's waiting to be selected to play this game.

The prosecutor approaches him, but keeps some distance as her normal wall of security is behind the beast. He's big, but he could be fast. "I understand you're prepared to relate the occurrences on Saturday the 14th of October?"

Jake shifts, causing the courtroom's occupants to hold their breath. "Yes, ma'am. Where should I start?" His voice is deep and smooth, like a dependable river that is never too high or low, but whose current is somehow still not worthy of trust. There is an undertow to him, a thing that will pull you down and never let you go.

His manners impress and confuse her, so she gives the floor to him. "Why don't you start at the beginning, Mr. Ryan?"

"Well, there comes a time in training where the weights aren't enough, they've done all they can do. And then the serious bodybuilders like me start looking into alternate methods of growth. We begin to consider the things that were once unthinkable to us devotees of the natural way to build.

"For a while you can still claim "natty," still convince the kids beneath you that you aren't juicing. But one day you wake up and you look in the mirror and it's like you never even knew you could grow so huge. And it's obvious to everyone--your wife, your mom, your doctor, the bros at the front desk of your gym-- yeah, you're on that good old performance enhancer. And they're gonna hate you for it and tell you you're gonna die sooner and all that shit. But fuck it, you look insane and they're just too chicken shit to try it. I know it's illegal, but I'm here already, so I'm gonna tell the whole story."

"That's good. That's what we want. Tell us what happened." She sits on the corner of the table designated to her and her clients, the parents of the deceased. They scowl at him, the man who was supposed to protect their daughter.

"When the first package came I was nervous. Worried some cops would break my door down or that I'd be injecting motor oil instead of testosterone. I'd get some kind of result from the contents of the box in front of me, but I wasn't sure if it'd be the results I wanted. I held that tiny needle in my giant hands and I really felt like I was standing on the edge of a cliff. And I stood on that edge for a good half hour. Behind was the old me, ahead was my unfulfilled destiny. This was gonna change everything, ya know?"

The prosecutor nods, thinking he wants confirmation, but his 'ya know' is only a storytelling device, a rhetorical question. The man and his ego have no interest in other's opinions.

"I couldn't pussy out. There's a lot of pressure in that world to be macho. I refused to be the guy who shied from a needle. That first time I pinned, I was scared as shit, but as soon as I'd injected I felt better and then great. It was potent stuff, this euphoric kinda feeling came with it. In a matter of weeks, that gear changed my life. I was killing my personal records left and right, lifting weights I'd never dreamed of. I felt like a god, unstoppable and limitless. My girl and I were fucking like rabbits and she even helped me pin. My needs were insatiable. It felt like I'd found a fucking fountain of youth. I was the epitome of the alpha male."

"If things were so great, why are we here today?" The prosecutor asked, but with some regret after the female of her clients, the mother of the victim, began to cry. The attorney could have allowed the monster to ramble for a while longer, as his sense of self-importance was no doubt capable of dominating a conversation and room for hours.

The beast shook his head. "Ya know, roid rage is a real thing, at least for me anyway. I woke up one day, tripped on a dog toy and I lost my fucking mind. I broke half our dishware and one of the bathroom mirrors over a fucking stubbed toe and a slightly bruised ego. She was out that day walking the dog. I was grateful for that once I'd calmed down and saw the damage I'd done."

"How did she react when she and the dog came home?"

"She cleaned it all up, bandaged my hands. Even went out and bought a mirror we could use temporarily until a contractor could replace the one in the bathroom. She cooked me dinner."

"So," the prosecutor stood and addressed the jurors, "like a good wife?"

"Yes, there was no better wife than her." He hangs his head and looks at the palms of his hands. Large callouses line up in rows beneath his fingers, testament to his hours of dedication in a gym.

"Were things different from then on?"

"After that first incident, I was extremely testy. I couldn't keep my shit together. From that moment on, I couldn't stay calm. I'd cry over movies. I threatened to kill our neighbors over overflowing trash bins. I spent more and more time at the gym. I was obsessed with chasing that ideal physique. Guys I'd admired started asking me for advice. It was this strange mix of good and bad. I was sure any of the gods of the industry had suffered through similar highs and lows, so I stuck with it, even upped my doses."

"And how did your wife feel about the mood swings, the increased time away from home?"

"She noticed it was changing me and she begged me to stop, but the results I was seeing in the mirror, I couldn't turn away from those. Once you've tasted that power, you'll give up a lot to not go back to being average. I was looking to the future of my bodybuilding career. Sponsorships, maybe competitions if I really focused. My muscles were gonna take me somewhere. She could have come along for the ride."

"What other types of changes did you see?"

"Well, I had to take more supplements to counteract the health issues that can come with steroid use. My hair growth was as fucked up as my emotions. I started a weekly waxing regimen to keep it under control. I had to pay the Chinese chick extra. I mean, it was just so much hair, everywhere. I had buddies that I knew who were juicing too, that I could've asked about the side effects, but my pride was too strong. I didn't want to sound like a pussy who couldn't stomach his milk."

"Was your wife concerned about any of this?"

"She wanted me to see the doctor, but I knew what he'd say and I wasn't going to listen anyway. She stopped helping me pin. We fought often about it. Each fight was worse. I hit her once, when she trashed my steroids and my protein. Told her to move out. She should have."

"Tell me about the day that it happened."

"She was home that day. The dog was sick so she called out of work. I woke up, showered, noticed all the new hair that had come in overnight. It clogged the tub drain. When I got out of the shower, my feet landed in dog shit. I yelled for the dog, who blindly obeyed and came in with his head down. I picked him up by the neck and shook him as I yelled in his face. He whimpered and then he stopped. His squirming gave me a pump. My biceps were bulging, the veins had never been so pronounced. They disappeared as more and more hair grew. I was still naked, standing in front of the double mirrors in our bedroom, admiring my body, when she came in and saw the dog's body. And then she saw me. Something was different. My eyes were yellow. I couldn't see any skin beneath all the hair. My muscles were insanely huge. I felt like I would burst out of my own skin. I heard her heart quicken. I smelled her blood and fear. In the back of my mind, I knew she was scared and sad about the dog, but I wanted to..um...taste her blood. And I didn't just want to taste it, I wanted to be covered in it. My jaw hurt. I thought maybe I'd been clenching it, which I've done in the gym when I get hyperfocused on a workout, but I looked in the mirror and saw the fangs. More of me was changing before my eyes. I heard her tell me to calm down.

"But you didn't calm down?"

"No."

"What did you do?"

"I picked her up and shook her like the dog."

"Ladies and gentlemen of the juror, those viewing the proceedings, I'm about to show very graphic images of what this man did to his wife."

The lights dim and a slide projector clicks on. A portable screen shows ten images of a once white bedroom turned red with blood and littered with unidentifiable pieces of a human. Jake closes his eyes, too familiar with the carnage. Months have passed, but he can still taste her blood.

"You're an animal!" his mother-in-law screams. She runs at him, driven by maternal rage. A security guard meets her halfway, picks her up at the waist, and removes her from the courtroom.

"I will ask you again, what did you do to your wife?"

"I...I...I tore her apart."

"You did more than tear her apart." The prosecutor has gained courage and is looking into the eyes of the man who dismantled his beloved. A final photo is shown on the screen. It's him, but barely; his face is hairy and elongated, his eyes yellow, his fur matted with blood.

"I ate her."

"You devoured her." The prosecutor once again turns to the jurors. "My fellow human beings, this man, this beast, ate so much of his wife that what was left of her could be presented as evidence in a one gallon ziplock bag. But we're kinder than he is and won't subject you to that exhibit."

"Your honor, that photo is doctored. There's no way my client could transform into, what, a werewolf? That's ridiculous!" A thin, balding man breaks his silence from the defendant's table.

"When provoked, under the right conditions, we have video evidence of this change. Under great duress and threat to his safety, an independent dentist retrieved bite samples of his teeth in his transformed state. They match what little samples we obtained from the bone scraps of his wife," the prosecutor counters.

"Will you be showing video of this transformation? I'm sure we're all a little curious, to say the least."

"No, your honor. We feel his admittance to the crime is enough to compel the jury to sentence him for murder. The video is far more disturbing than the images shown. It...challenges what we know. We won't be showing it."

"Very well." The judge addresses the beast on the bench. "Is that the end of your testimony?"

"Yes, your honor."

"How do you plead, Mr. Ryan?"

"It was the steroids. It wasn't me. The side effects turned me into something I'm not."

"Answer the question. How do you plead?"

"Not guilty, sir. Not guilty."

Behind closed doors, the jury spends little time arguing over his guilt. They set a record, in fact, of twenty minutes. And most of that time is used waiting in line at a coffee vending machine.

Back in the courtroom, the lead juror stands up, wishing an electrified fence stood between him and the orange-suited killer. Something to keep even the largest of predators at bay. Jurassic Park-like, before the power grid went down.

"Has the jury reached a verdict?" The judge asks him.

"Yes, your honor. We the jury, after short discussion, have found Mr. Ryan to be...guilty as charged."

Beneath his jumpsuit, Jake's blood begins to boil. Hair sprouts from every pore and reaches for the loose weave of the cheap fabric covering it. The power is intoxicating.

"Furthermore," the juror continues, "we feel his obsessive nature and short fuse pose an extreme danger to society. This is a man who may snap again with little prompting. He is a threat."

Jake sees his vision change. Details of every movement become clearer. A scratched chin, a shifted position, each and every blink of an eye. His sense of smell enhances. Every scent in the room greets him for consideration. The perfumes and soaps, the wax used to polish all the wood, the dirty assess. Some blood smells sweeter. He can smell the fear, as those nearest his bench have begun to notice the change. His ears pick up on quickening heartbeats.

"Mr. Ryan?" The prosecutor addresses him. "Please remain calm."

His breathing labors, as though he's run a

marathon. It shifts to a low growl as the bone and muscle of his jaw realign into a more damaging bite. He drops to his knees on the floor in front of the bench and pulls his wrists apart until the metal links of the cuffs break.

"Guards!" The judge stands up, ready to make a move for the safety of his chambers if necessary.

The seam on the back of his jumpsuit splits open, exposing a muscular, fur covered back. He turns and grips the wooden bench with both of his giant, bear like hands, and swings it around to meet one of the approaching officers in the head.

□

A month later, the wounds from both bullets gifted him at his trial have already completely healed. No scars remain. Jake takes the quick route to solitary by eating his cellmate after the man's failed attempt to assert dominance. The rumors spread quickly following the incident: cannibal, canine, creature. Then, when the prison sees opportunity to benefit from the beast serving life without possibility of parole, he gets wheeled away to a private lab for tests. They muzzle him, taunt him, provoke the monster hiding beneath the surface. His blood is drawn, hair samples taken, fangs and claws removed. It all grows back. They feed him more steroids. They feed him live animals. Watch him workout. Pad his canteen fund until it bulges like his muscles.

Jake can't decide if it's heaven or hell. All he ever wanted to do was get paid to workout. But not like this. Not when it seems like they're building his body for a war.

THE MADNESS COIL

"Does it hurt when I press here?" The doctor asks. His exam is not thorough, not comprehensive, which Lora will pay for later. A little more digging and he might find the deeper issue, the crack in the cement barely holding back the floodwaters. But he is too young to do more than gently touch the mottled skin around the stitches and nod appraisingly. He is still in his residency and unsure of his knowledge or position. His is a generic opinion.

"No, not really," the repaired woman replies after a successfully stifled laugh, because she is ticklish, not because self-inflicted stab wounds are humorous. She pulls down her shirt to cover her belly. The sterile paper of the exam table crinkles as she moves and it sounds like the thin sheets you use to choose a doughnut or protect your thighs and ass from filthy public toilet seats. She'd rather be doing either of those things, with no preference for one or the other.

"I don't think you can expect scarring of any noticeable amount, Lora." He knows enough to not make promises, but to speak with authority nonetheless. It's a fine line determined by tone and word choice, and marred by lawsuits.

"That's great, honey," Manny, Lora's boyfriend, celebrates, but only briefly. He needs the doctor's opinion. "Doctor, may I speak with you privately?"

Nora knows what this is about, but she doesn't believe the details and she refuses to watch the video. Manny doesn't need to ask her to leave either. She steps out of the examination room and finds her way through the maze of hallways, avoiding the urge to snoop at other patients' charts tossed into plexiglass holders along the route. Surely these untouchable breadcrumbs would betray that someone has it worse off than she. In the waiting area, magazines promise her solutions to all life's banal issues, but there's no lipstick shade that'll match her level of losing it, no skirt in this year's trendy floral quite high-waisted enough to hide her crazy, even if the wound heals without a scar. She settles on a crossword at the back of a gossip magazine and fishes a pen from her purse. Someone before her has taken the same risk, in permanent blue instead of black, but she shakes her head at their incorrect, sloppy inscription. Four letter word for *precipice*. The cruciverbalist guessed *wall*, not a bad choice, but it won't work with the surrounding answers. A pain explodes in her back, which she grimaces through and writes off as healing-related. *Edge*, that's the obvious answer, and so she asserts her dominance in black upon black of redrawn letters to hide the mistake.

□

Manny holds his cell phone as steady as possible while the doctor watches the footage. He turns the volume up hesitantly, aware that patients and staff in adjacent rooms could hear the madness if he isn't careful. In the video, the phone is propped on something and looking into a dining room. Lora sits at a table, a knife and fork in hands.

"MEAT! MEAT! MEAT!" The yell is guttural, cavewoman-esque, and desperate in its demand "CALVIN WANTS MEAT!" She bellows as she slams the silverware into the wood.

Manny slides a t-bone, barely cooked, still dripping blood, onto the plate in front of his girlfriend. "Here you go, dear."

She drops the cutlery and attacks the cut with hands, teeth, and a starving fervor that leave nothing but the bone to fall on the plate.

"It was the third steak that night," Manny explains. I set up my phone when the voices started, after the first one."

The steak knife is back in her hand. She lifts her shirt and rotates the sharp metal with purpose, like a dowsing rod finding water, to point at her flesh.

The doctor watches Manny rush in front of the phone's camera, but Lora plunges the blade into her side before he can reach her. Three inches of penetration, a barely missed major organ, the doctor knows that Lora is lucky, but for both she and Manny, it is only the beginning of a long, and possibly endless journey.

Manny kills the video, shoves his phone in a jacket pocket, and rubs an ache in his forehead. "She doesn't remember any of it. I don't know what to do. Who the hell is Calvin?"

The doctor cannot call her crazy, cannot use the words jumping around in his brain. He must maintain professionalism. He must be helpful and delicate. "I have a friend, a psychiatrist. She's familiar with these types of...illnesses." He points at his head as he says 'these types.' Manny knows it'll be difficult getting that gesture out of his mind.

"That's a bit much, don't you think? After one incident? She's never had any of these outbursts before. Ever." But she had been talking to herself a lot. More than her usual work mode banter that was purely a thinking out loud to oneself. Lora wasn't talking about articles and ideas anymore, she was discussing escape from somewhere, and "the next plans."

"That's even more troubling, Manny. A sudden onset of behavioral changes, accompanied by self-harm? Lora needs a mental evaluation immediately."

He walks his troubled, crossword-triumphant girlfriend to their car. She grips the torn out square of completed puzzle in a fist. Proof of life in her addled brain. He considers admonishing her for the property damage, but instead focuses on the half of a celebrity's face peering from the other side of the crumpled paper. He can't come up with the man's name no matter where he digs in his memory, but the challenge is a welcome distraction. Around them, other non-famous people open doors for mendable loved ones who didn't stab themselves in the gut, who didn't receive referrals to psychiatrists.

Tomorrow frightens him and the day after that, more so. He met Lora in college, where they were both studying literature, and he fell for her brilliant mind almost immediately. If something brain-altering is happening, the part of Lora he loves most might not survive. Doors, he could open for a lifetime, but he wouldn't change adult diapers, couldn't keep the Suicide Hotline on speed dial. It just wasn't in him.

□

The day of Lora's mental evaluation, just four days after the doctor stitched her closed, hasn't come soon enough. Grey half moons hang beneath Manny's eyes, pulling years from his face like tides. He skips his shave, deciding the stubble better pairs with the shadows and the overall feeling of fuck-it-all that comes with rounding up your girlfriend for a trip to the shrink. He was used to Lora's late nights, the ones where she sat in the glow of her antique Tiffany lamp, taking notes in books for future papers. But her nocturnal habits have changed. The soft light now traded for the complete dark and her quiet focus, for frenzied arguments with herself. Or whomever she's been talking to.

And now in his nowhere-near-rested daze, he's searching the house for her. He imagines she's overthinking her psych evaluation outfit, flinging ancient, flowing skirts, and much-too-revealing tops aside for something more professional and sane looking. Wasting hours in the walk-in closet, because honestly, crazy cannot be tucked into jeans, skinny or otherwise. When she isn't there, he heads downstairs to the kitchen, where she and coffee would be working on taming her jitters, if she even has mind enough to be nervous. And sure enough, he can smell the dark roast brewing.

Lora has selected black yoga pants, dark sunglasses, and an oversized grey hoodie, which reminds Manny of the go-to outfit of celebs fresh out of rehab or plastic surgery. But she isn't going anywhere because she is on the floor of the kitchen, writhing and sliding on the newly-laid linoleum. At first it looks like a seizure, but there is a controlled purpose to her movements.

"Lora, what are you doing?"

He hated the flooring when she picked it out. The bland beige of it wasn't a proper match to the color of the cabinets. It dated the entire house, made the incompatible browns of the kitchen look like mixed nuts to him. He hates it even more now that his girlfriend is crawling around on the tragedy.

She pulls the sunglasses from her face and her eyes burn into him as she raises an accusing finger to point. "WHY DID YOU HIDE THE KNIVES? MALACHI WANTS TO PLAY!"

Malachi is the exact reason he hid the knives, and the pills, and anything else that could kill. This personality is dangerous, dominant, and angry. He is everything Manny's girlfriend is not.

"'Malachi, let me talk to Lora." His voice shakes. He is a powerless child, standing at the open door of a neighbor's home, staring up at a powerful parent, begging to play with his friend and not even knowing if she is inside.

"LORA HATES YOU HATES YOU HATES YOU!" His girlfriend curls into a tight ball in front of the oven. Dust and crumbs from their normal life cling to her dark spandex tights, mimicking the print of a more suitable selection for a mental review. The coffee pot screams that it's done and Manny wholeheartedly agrees.

He pulls her from the floor and the fetal position. She struggles against him, arms and legs akimbo, akin to a toddler in tantrum or a drunken, aggressive friend. Everywhere. Getting in too many clean swings for someone so uncaffeinated and out of control. Her hair has come out of the ponytail she placed it in. All the twisting and chaos rolled the rubber band off, leaving her with reinstated bedhead.

□

As the car warms up, the engine heat makes slow growing holes in the ice on the windshield and Lora cries. She regrets choosing the weather-inappropriate yoga pants, but butterflies or something equally busy jump inside her stomach and anything more fitting for her form or the situation was too snug over the discomfort. Manny pulls a lint roller, normally reserved for dress wear, from the glove compartment and drops it in her lap for the crumbs still clinging to her legs. She wonders if this is when relationships begin to die, when he doesn't even take the fuzz-covered, used sheet off the roll for her. When she doesn't say "thanks for thinking of the crumbs, I hadn't noticed" or "thanks for picking up the pieces of me from our kitchen floor, I don't recall falling apart there." She shivers and thinks of the coffee left to die in the pot. Manny drives. She tears the used layer from the roll and tosses the sticky ball to the floor. There's something about unmarred black fabric that makes her feel fancy, unbreakable, and upper class, but today, no matter how many miniscule outsiders she pulls from the cloth, the effect isn't there. She's fading and wearing thin in places, like her pants washed and worn too many times.

□

The front lawn is a picture-perfect, demented dreamscape, a Hieronymus Bosch masterpiece come to life. Orderlies attempt to wrangle wandering patients who are off in their own worlds. The grass is a utilitarian short and tidy, maybe even Astroturf, and greener than she recalls grass being. Occasional benches offer physical respite. Random screams scatter nicely with the chirping of the birds. Lora can't imagine herself a part of this circus. She and Manny walk the path that cuts through the psychotic serenity and leads directly to the front doors. Never in Lora's life, even while attending an ancient stone college, has a building loomed so threateningly high above her.

The threshold is a wall she fears scaling, as though crossing it will mean she can never go back to her old life again. A one way door. A choice that can't be taken back. The first step to admitting she has a problem. She leaves the stable earth and sinks into the quicksand of her mental instability, unable to escape her reality now that both feet are on the scuffed white floors of the psychiatric hospital. All she can hope is that they won't admit her, won't turn her out into the field to age and die like the other cattle.

□

Lora sits on a hard, metal chair and looks with disdain at the stark white, artless walls surrounding her. The cold of the chair touches her through the thinness of her pants. She pulls her sweater close to her body in a hug as she catches a glimpse of her reflection in her sunglasses she has set on the table. The extra fabric feels like a straight jacket, and her messy hair looks like a permanent, gravity-defying backcomb. The epitome of psych ward chic. She isn't even sure how it got so screwed up in the first place. It won't aid her case, but the idea to fix it with spit and palm doesn't cross her mind.

A clock ticks from somewhere in the room, but she finds no inspiration to locate the source. Her body twitches to the rhythm, like rippling water in a bowl beneath a leaky faucet. Each tremor agitates her further and the man across from her is asking too many questions she doesn't know the answers to.

"What do you remember about the steak knife incident?" He's keeping the beat of the second hand with his pen, dropping it on a pad of paper like a sideways pendulum.

Lora feels nauseated. "Only the pain afterward. And I was full of food. So there was pain from that too."

"You don't recall eating three t-bones and then

stabbing yourself with a steak knife?"

"No and why would I want to?" Something stirs inside of her.

"Your husba-"

"He's my boyfriend."

"He has video of the event."

"I don't want to see it. I believe what he told me. That's good enough for me."

"Have you ever heard voices other than your own inside of your head?"

Lora nearly wishes she does, just to give the man a bone. Her vision darkens and her arms fall to her sides. She bursts forward, snatches the pen from his hand, and draws a line on one side of his neck before he can pull away. A guard rushes in and handcuffs her to the chair. He makes no move to leave.

"You can go. I'm fine," the evaluator assures the guard. He feels his neck for ink and blood. It isn't his first close encounter with a troubled individual.

"I'D LIKE TO TASTE HIM!" Lora growls.

"SHUT UP MALACHI. HE WANTS TO HEAR US! HE WANTS TO LISTEN!"

"CALVIN IS SO QUIET TODAY."

"WE SHOULD HAVE SLICED HIS NECK!"

Her head rolls back and she speaks again, but her voice is sharp and high and sounds nothing like Lora or the other voices.

"HELLO."

"Who am I speaking with now?"

"IT'S CYNTHIA. I LIKE IT IN HERE."

"How old are you, Cynthia?" He writes her name down beneath Malachi, Unknown, and Calvin, and waits to know more.

"I'M NEW! I'M NEW!"

"Does new mean you're small, you're young?"

Lora's head pulls upright and she grips the arms of the chair. "WE WANT OUT!" her voice bellows. "THERE'S NO MORE ROOM. TOO MANY! TOO MANY!"

□

An hour and a half later, Manny sits in a slightly more furnished room, free to move about if he wishes, of no threat to anyone. Anxiety courses through him. His feet dance with nervous seizure on the carpet, which is the same bummed out beige as the kitchen linoleum at home. He could easily see Lora slithering around in here, acting like a maniac, but he has to keep those bizarre thoughts in check if he wants to help her. He wonders where they are keeping her and why her evaluation wasn't done in this room.

Across from Manny, a psychiatrist-with more years under his professional belt than their medical doctor has lived-scruffs his tangled beard and frowns as he reviews his notes. He looks up and manages to speak through the scowl and the facial hair. "In the first hour, my colleague has identified seven unique personalities, but we think there may be as many as fourteen."

No lead up. No lube to help the news slide in painlessly. "Fourteen?" He wanted just his one Lora, one was enough. "Where do we go from here? What are we dealing with?"

"Schizophrenia, possibly. It's a little early to tell, but she's exhibiting many of the symptoms. I can start her on an antipsychotic and we can go from there."

"Are we safe, at home?" He secretly hopes they'll keep her for the night, for observation. If he misses anymore sleep, he'll qualify for a deprivation study and the circles under his eyes will become a fixture on his face.

"I believe with the medication and an edited environment, she won't pose a risk to anyone."

"Edited?"

"Essentially child safe. Nothing sharp, looped, electrified, deep, poisonous...do you understand what I'm saying?"

Nothing that could kill. Thankfully he'd already done that and thank god they didn't have children. Both he and Lora had wanted them at a time, but school, work, and life in general always got in the way. No, she was only a threat to herself and to him, and he could leave if his life depended on it. They were only bound together through a rental agreement, a joint bank account that he mostly controlled, and a few home decor selections he could live without, including that god awful brown kitchen. Marriage was a distant thought.

□

At the drugstore, Lora stays in the car, spectacle enough without picking up a prescription for antipsychotics. Somehow she's warm, even in the tights and the cold. The windows fog up and she welcomes the anonymity that the newly opaque glass affords her.

Manny stands at the pharmacist's counter, listening to the side effects and usage instructions for the pills, the newest member of their family, the miniature white elephant in the room. His attention shifts to an anti-smoking poster and he considers picking up a pack. He smoked when he and Lora met, but it turned her off of kissing him. Cold turkey would have been hard if it weren't for her lips on his. He can't remember the last time he kissed her now. Weeks at least.

"Sir? Are you listening?" The pharmacist is shaking the paper bag in front of his face, which he thinks is rude, but so is tuning out a drug presentation to think about cigarettes you shouldn't touch and making out with your girlfriend back when you were in college.

"Yeah, yeah I am. Sorry. It's all just a bit much to handle lately. These are for my girlfriend and she isn't doing well."

"If she's needing these, she definitely isn't doing well at all. But they should help. Give it a few weeks. Everything I said is on this sheet stapled to the bag. Read it when your head clears and hang in there."

51

Manny leaves feeling like he wants more for hanging in there. A gold star sticker or a pat on the back from the man behind the counter. A night off from the madness. Anything.

□

A week later, Lora stares at her hand, envisioning one of her favorite pens cradled there; a phantom limb of her literary life. She isn't allowed the puncturing tools of her trade. It's all computer work if she wants to write or research. Manny has even replaced the cabled keyboard with one that works via wireless Bluetooth. She isn't interested in dying, but no one believes a woman who has pierced a hole in herself. With an increase in the frequency of the blackouts, her work begins to suffer. She hasn't finished an article in weeks.

It doesn't seem like the drugs are helping anything, except to increase Manny's paranoia. Never did he think he'd be sneaking moments alone with the medicine cabinet in the bathroom, running the sink faucet to cover the noise of pills rattling against orange plastic, but he must be sure Lora is taking the drugs. He lines the tablets up and runs a quick head count, the only roll call where the sergeant will be happy to find a few soldiers missing. Good. Two more gone, off fighting the good fight in her body. There are changes in her behavior, but not any he is expecting to see. She sleeps more, but the voices talk in her sleep, whisper things he can't understand. And though she has tried to hide it, he can tell she's gaining weight.

Water collects in the tub at Lora's feet, rising imperceptibly at first. When it reaches her ankles, she kicks a foot back and tests the drain plug with a toe to make sure it hasn't popped closed. It's open, but her toe brings back a clump of hair, like seaweed, dangling and limp with water. As she turns to face the drain, something shifts inside her body, propelling her forward and then onto her knees. Surrounding the drain, clumps of her thick hair have formed an effective dam. She picks up the mounds, allowing the water to escape at it's normal pace.

"Manny!" She yells as she pulls more hair from her head.

It isn't Lora's patchy hair that shocks him. It's her naked body. Manny hasn't seen it for two weeks and it's unrecognizable as hers. Not even her hands look as they had. Everything is bloated, misshapen, and wrong. She hardly looks human.

"Why the hell didn't you tell me, Lora?"

"I thought it might be a side effect of the medication."

"Come on, you're not an idiot. You know this isn't normal."

"And I didn't want you to worry."

"But now you let me in on the secret? Just had to make sure I got the full effect?"

She holds up palms full of hair. "I can't hide this."

"Give me that." He takes the hair and Lora sees

it as a sweet gesture, but the feeling passes when he drops the wet balls into the trash like mashed potatoes being slopped onto a plate. He hands her a towel and her pills. "Dry off and we can eat lunch."

□

"Her condition is deteriorating!" Each word comes out in increasingly slower motion. Manny has heard the same words, in the exact same order, shouted by actors playing doctors in movie set emergency rooms. But never has he spoken these words until now. The secretary he has reached is not impressed by the show.

"LET US OUT! LET US OUT!" Lora screeches from behind him. She is not strapped to a stretcher, or gurney, or hospital bed, nor is she attached to reality. She is naked and he has trapped her in the pantry after she tried to strangle him with a towel.

"There's no more time. The medication isn't doing anything for the voices. They're worse, in fact!" The offending towel is on the floor at his feet, it's perfect white making the brown tile look even more atrocious. At this very moment, his entire life seems like a bad idea, like something that should be lit on fire and walked away from.

"WE'LL FIND A WAY TO GET YOU!" She screams, then goes quiet.

Manny hears a bag being ripped open, the telltale scattering of chips across the tile floor, and then crunching.

"Physically she's different too. These aren't side

effects. She needs to be seen immediately." He wanted to yell "I'm losing her!" because how could anyone come back from so much treading water at the deepest end of the pool? Who could save his drowning Lora? He wouldn't be able to grip her chubby, waterlogged hands to keep her above the surface anyway. He'd sooner let go than live in an environment so "edited" that bath towels are banned over threat of linen ligatures. The woman on the phone, after warning him to lower his voice, which he didn't, has hung up.

If screaming at the top of your lungs after attempting murder isn't exhausting enough, eating an entire bag of sour cream and onion potato chips must be a sedative. Manny removes the chair blocking the pantry door, turns the knob, and allows gravity to lower Lora's sleeping form onto the floor. He drags her and stray chips into the kitchen proper, an act requiring all of his strength and energy. She lies there like a bleached, beached whale on the verge of explosion from the gases of efficient decay or the dynamite of do-good men. He imagines gulls picking at her and eventually, bone collectors. A death with purpose. And sometime in that process, scientists will come along and examine her, take samples of organs and stomach contents to determine a cause of death. And they'll present those findings to the newspapers, which will print a picture of her sand-hugged, collapsing body under the giant headline: What Killed Her. But Manny will read it as: What Killed Us.

□

Lora brushes her teeth, rinses with mouthwash,

repeats, but nothing kills her oniony breath. Manny told her she had a violent fit and explained why she wound up naked on the kitchen floor. None of it makes sense. She dresses in the one item that still fits, a Hawaiian print muumuu given to her on her 40th birthday as a gag gift for being over the hill. In the back of the closet, she grabs a straw hat from a bin full of Halloween decorations. Normal her might silently thank the scarecrow she is borrowing it from, but humor doesn't exist anymore, not when you've eaten an entire bag of chips in the nude after trying to strangle your boyfriend. The hat hides her bald dome, the Velcro of her adjustable Tevas obliges her cankles and the other hills of her fattened feet. Her outfit could pass as normal if an island stretched out underfoot and the sun shone overhead. If it weren't February in cold, wet Seattle. But it is mid-winter and the frost on the ground spits at her skin as she crushes it. Thousands of angry snakes in the grass.

□

Manny doesn't look up as she labors into the car, first sitting sideways on the seat with her feet resting on the sidewalk, and then the slow rotation to bring her entire body inside, like a carousel beset with off-season rust, moaning and creaking back to orbital life. When he hears the door close, he turns the car engine over. Lora struggles with her seatbelt and Manny, with impatience. He rips the belt from her hands, shoves it between Lora's thigh and the center console, and reaches blindly for the lock end.

"Suck in or something."

She does her best, but there isn't much room in her lumpy, distended belly for anything to move. It's just enough for him to force it to click in. The belt strap digs into Lora's belly, making her look like a roast tied up for baking. Manny wipes sweat from his brow. Even in the cold of the morning, the inside of the car feels like an oven. Heat emanates off her swollen body, as does the scent of sour cream and onion potato chips.

Since college, since even before college, Lora was a stunner. He'd had a difficult time piecing together how someone as gorgeous as her was also intelligent and kind. She truly was a complete package and somehow she wanted him, a book nerd covered in hair and full of bad ideas. Now though, it would appear to a stranger that he was doing her a favor by granting her a relationship.

He drives, running red lights and through various conversational scenarios in his mind. There will be an exchange of words, because they don't have an appointment. He'd been demanding one for a week. The windows are down despite the crisp air.

□

"We need to see Dr. Spruce, right now!"

The receptionist is staring at Lora, who is staring at the receptionist's half-eaten sausage links like they're made of gold. "I'm sorry, sir. You'll need to make an appointment."

"No appointments! No more waiting!" Manny opens his arms to present his sideshow freak girlfriend like a new car in an ad or Vanna White showcasing letters on Wheel of Fortune. But this one is an unfortunate lemon, a loss, a downward spiral of no more vowels and definitely no more of the "s's". The entire wheel is made up of bankruptcies.

"There are emergency rooms for these situations."

Manny shakes his head. "Have you heard of YouTube? If I take her to an emergency room, every tween there will have her posted online to be mocked. No. No!"

Lora can't discern if Manny's concern over publicity is truly selfless as he claims, or if he just doesn't want to be filmed sitting next to her.

The cacophony brings the young doctor out and seeing Lora is enough for him to direct his secretary to cancel his other appointments for the day. Back in a small room, she has downgraded her tropical muumuu from adornment to a brightly colored pile on a chair. Her bare feet bear angry, red depressions where the Velcro straps fought to maintain closure. She dons the provided gown, but can't reach to tie it closed. Her back bulges from the gap. One size fits most, many, maybe. But not at all when your entire life has shrunk in the wash. The doctor performs a complete physical, including x-rays and ultrasounds.

Manny hangs back in the waiting room, feeling a small amount of guilt for how he's treated Lora and he resolves to take her somewhere nice when her ordeal ends. He can still smell the potato chips. He might need to find a new favorite flavor. After the exam, Lora trades places with Manny. Most people would insist on being in the room for a diagnosis, but she simply can't stomach any news. Manny can filter it for her, make it more palatable. He follows the scent of onion to an exam room.

□

"All right, Manny, have a seat. It's a good thing you brought her in."

"Thank you for seeing her. What's the news?"

"I'm happy to let you know that after the physical examination, we've rejected the multiple personality diagnosis. It isn't schizophrenia or any other mental illness."

Manny claps his hands. Finally some good news. His life might be safe from an all-consuming blaze after all. "That's wonderful, but what's really going on with her?"

"Well, we've found several anomalies in the scans that I wanted to discuss with you."

"Anomalies? Are those tumors? Can cancer affect the brain and body like this?"

"It's not cancer. She is healthy, physically and mentally, even though she doesn't look that way."

"Okay, I'm not following."

"I'm just going to show you. It'll explain everything."

Lora sits in the waiting room, losing herself

in the pale sage of the walls. She has a good eye for interior design, she thinks, but it never quite translates at home. She blames the mismatched kitchen on poor service and lighting at the home repair store. Her fingers trace the outlines of the hibiscus flowers on her dress. A pregnant woman waiting for another physician, and sitting across from her, smiles. *I understand what it feels like to be bursting at the seams. I know what it means to never be full.* But your baby doesn't threaten to kill your boyfriend, or you, Lora wants to say. Whatever is inside of her aims to burst from her chest like a multi-limbed alien. What she wouldn't give to be able to push the bullshit out of her crotch and be done with it.

She picks up a bit of dry reading material from a chipped side table and contemplates the rigorous vetting process the magazines must go through to make the cut and end up mostly ignored here. Mental Health Weekly has a crossword puzzle, she discovers, but someone has filled in every blank with the letter 'S' and then scribbled over the entire page. Deciding it will drive her crazier to have nothing to focus on while she waits, she attempts to read through the tangles of ink and answer the clues in her mind.

□

Manny crosses the waiting room, taking everyone in before looking at Lora. They are already watching his girlfriend. Her eyes are fixed on the fish tank set in the wall across from her, while she scratches her fingers on her thighs in squiggly lines from knees to hips, over and over. A magazine lies open on the floor at her feet.

"Lora!" He stands in front of her gaze and places his hands on hers to calm her movements.

""WE ALMOST BROKE FREE!" She whispers in a voice that isn't hers.

"Lora!" he yells this time, unconcerned for the small audience behind him. YouTube be damned, he finally had an answer and things might be okay. "Look at me, honey."

She raises her eyes from the fixed point of fish tank-turned-sweater, in control again. She cannot discern the bags under his eyes, for the rest of his face is just as grey. He steps to the side, exposing the magazine he has been standing on. Lora picks it up and shows him the ink-mangled puzzle.

The crossword alarms him. He isn't sure how to approach the chaotic lines, so he takes it from her and returns the issue to the table near her chair. He puts the magazine at the bottom of the pile, buries it like he hopes he can the rest of these memories.

"I solved it. In record time!" She points at her head with swollen fingers reddened from scratching, just as the doctor had gestured after she stabbed herself, and Manny's concern for her mental health comes rushing back. Lora doesn't explain the pen wasn't her, that she solved it all in her head despite the squid ink pasta art someone else so rudely left behind. He's staring now, at her and how grotesque she has become, and even though he can't see them, he's staring at the things inside her.

"Manny, does the doctor have an answer? Can

he help me?"

"I think it's better that you see for yourself."

□

Lora hobbles down the hallways as though she planned them, so familiar with the path and the paintings that she can call the turns and brushstrokes before they're in view. The nurse directs them into Exam Room Three and leaves them with instructions to wait for the doctor. Lora spends a few minutes trying to squish into the chair next to Manny, but opts to sidle onto the exam table when the chair arms prove too narrow for her new bulk.

She tears at the paper beneath her. Her body feels busy, in constant motion, alive with a continuous hum of activity. But there is no cosmic beauty in the energy. It is vengeful movement, an alignment of stars and plans for evil deeds, and a thing that most definitely cannot end well. Lora knows she is a bomb about to go off, she just hasn't figured out what the explosion will look like.

□

A light, short knock on the door. If you are a normal person, it's just enough time to stop playing with the rubber gloves, speculating on the purpose of instruments clamped to the walls, and re-reading the informational posters placed between them on the flu virus and proper hand washing techniques. Lora looks like a Masker: bulbous, gaudily adorned, haphazardly made up to resemble the idea of a woman, not quite right. Sometime recently she'd shifted from earthly goddess to a near-human inhabitant of the uncanny valley. Manny knows what's in Lora's folder and therefore, what is inside of her, what this thing is playing in his woman's skin. He hasn't been normal since he'd gained that knowledge.

The young doctor is a reminder they need better health insurance, the kind where you can select your provider, but he is nonetheless a welcome break to the painful silence filling the chair Lora couldn't use.

He drops to a rolling stool procured from beside a counter and Lora watches as his shoulders continue the fall. He sighs and opens her file. "I'm going to show you an image of your abdomen and I don't want you to be alarmed." He pulls an x-ray or an ultrasound—or whatever it was they did to her in the gown that wouldn't close—from the folder and slaps it on the light box affixed to the wall.

Lora gasps and begins to cry. Her boyfriend holds her gently. She hopes no one snooped in her folder as she might have done. She shudders.

"IT'S US!" the voices hiss all at once.

Manny releases his hold on her. The doctor rolls backward. The voices have never spoken together before.

After a deep breath to regain composure, the doctor plucks a pen from a pocket on the chest of his shirt. He points with a weak arm to the image and the tubular shapes winding throughout her core. "These are tapeworms. Manny, that's who you've been hearing, who we just heard."

"I've seen tapeworms before. They weren't this big." Lora hopes for an explanation less disturbing than giant worms filling up her insides. "Where did they come from? Why are they this large?"

"How can they talk?" Manny asks. His girlfriend's lack of concern bewilders him, as that seems like the most pressing question. He didn't ask any questions when he first saw the images, before Lora was in the room. He was too stunned. Online, there are things-you-can't-unsee type videos of tapeworm removal, but those worms didn't look like this.

"Tapeworms, when untreated, can grow up to thirty feet long. It's likely you were exposed to them through the consumption of undercooked salmon. But these tapeworms are larger in diameter than usual. They are super-sized, which explains the pain. We, well, the CDC, will work on the sentience question."

"The CDC?"

"They monitor things like this. And since it appears your friends may have come from Japan, there's concern over radioactivity as well."

"How do we ki...get them out of me?" Lora watches her words because the worms understand them.

"There are several effective medications for treatment of tapeworms, but these are not average creatures. We may need to attempt surgical removal."

"Whatever we have to do to get them out of me. I want my life back. Our life." Lora looks at Manny, but he doesn't look back. Maybe there isn't a life to get back. Maybe she was right about the lint roller tape incident. Their relationship had reached terminal length. It would be a slow death from here.

"That's the real issue. If they feel threatened, they may attack you from the inside. This one here is wrapped around your spinal column. It could paralyze you if it decides that is beneficial to their survival. Others are threatening organs, like this one here. Inside its coil is a kidney. It's quite fascinating how they've adapted to life in other areas of the body."

"It's fucked up," Manny says. He closes his eyes and remembers the salmon. The restaurant was his pick. Lora wore a gorgeous summer dress of yellows and pinks. They joked that she blended into the delicate, Japanese upholstery behind her. He ordered the yakisoba and they drank a bottle of plum wine. The salmon was expensive, but he urged her to try it, convinced her it would be worth the cost. That smile, the sex that night, her renewed interest in their relationship, it all seemed worth it at the time. But had he known what was lying in wait in the fish, he would have swayed her to choose a less pricey item, something cooked to high heaven and back, a dish with no possible way of hosting another life form.

He is still at the restaurant in his memory, but Lora is fully present. "But they want out, right?" she verifies, still unable to recall anything the worms have said.

"It's not so easy. We don't know what kind of threat they pose once removed from your body. There's not an obvious course of action."

65

"We could starve them out," Lora suggests.

Manny shakes his head. "No, that's too dangerous."

"It's all dangerous, Manny," the doctor reminds him.

Another violent jolt takes Lora's body.

"IT'S RUDE TO TALK ABOUT SOMEONE IN THE ROOM!"

"WE CAN HEAR YOU!"

"IF WE GO, SHE GOES!"

"IT'S TIME TO SAY HELLO!"

Lora feels it, the wrongness of everything around her. A box of medium gloves sits empty on the wall. The doctor's pen is leaking in his jacket pocket. Manny doesn't love her anymore. The muumuu is out of season, out of region. The unchanged paper on the table sports greasy marks from someone else's body oil, or doughnut, or ass cheeks. She feels the wrongness in her body, the foreign agents making a swimming pool of her insides. She feels death. She stands up and turns to place her hands on the dirty exam table. Bent over, she struggles for breath. Without context, she could be a laboring women working on bringing an already beloved child into the world, thrown into the event in the wrong place. Tapeworms, like babies, arrive on their own schedule. The undulations overtake her.

"Manny, help me! The pressure! They're forcing their way out of me!" She screams.

The doctor has never heard such agony before,

but he learned about it once. He knows what it means for Lora, and what it could mean for him.

Manny stands behind her and holds her hips. Again without context he could be the supportive father repeating techniques learned in Lamaze classes. "Doctor, do something!"

There are few things to be done. The doctor rolls the stool backward and leaves the room. He doesn't specify the reason for his departure. Manny assumes it's to call an ambulance to take them to the emergency room, or to load a syringe with a sedative or painkiller or anything that will help Lora to be normal again, if even for a moment. But the doctor's stomach is weak and he knows he can claim ignorance and disassociate from the event if he isn't in the room when she dies.

The muumuu hides the chaos beneath her skin. Where there are no obvious, clear paths of exit, heads bore with sheer will through layers of muscle and fat. Her body is heavy in Manny's arms. The printed hibiscus flowers slip from his hands and fall to the floor. She exhales, long, drawn out, full of relief. No inhalation follows.

Now that she is still and the fabric lies flat on her body, Manny sees the boiling movements of the worms. Above the smiling neckline of the dress, a mound pulses; a tapeworm's mole-like push for the surface. At the other end of her body, between Lora's unmoving legs and beneath the floral hemline, something stirs.

MR. REAPER'S GHASTLY BOUTIQUE

The car dropped me off at the curb. The windows of the business in front of me were large, covered in condensation, and full of things organic and man-made. A sign hung above an imposing door of intricately-carved wood. I read the sign out loud.

"Mr. Reaper's Ghastly Boutique."

No other signs described the shop and no stickers boasted 'Free Wi-Fi', or 'Credit Cards Accepted', or 'Service Animals Welcome.' Not even a 'No Shirts, No Shoes, No Service.' The only other words on the front of the building were pasted above an equally ornate metal handle (some species of viper, it's body arched to form the grip, it's head and needle-sharp teeth craned in the direction of anyone attempting entry). The hand-written sign declared—somehow quite sternly—Private Clientele Only. I certainly wasn't a part of that exclusive list, but my name was plastered all over another list, one of the unemployment variety. Luckily, I'd been invited to the boutique for employment so I pressed down on the vipers upper jaw causing the door lock to unlatch, and despite any budding apprehension from gripping a likeness of a lethal snake, I entered.

Wood, leather, and metal things stacked in

precarious towers dominated the small shop. Many with gears and wheels, some with teeth. I call them things because most of them were new to me, unrecognizable as anything from normal life. To the right of the door, a tall, glass display case held dozens of bottles, each a different size, shape, and color. The sun shone through them, causing ethereal kites of amethyst, cerulean, coral, and fuchsia to blanket the space. The kaleidoscope only slightly softened the atmosphere of the bizarre, balmy room.

I heard rustling from behind a curtain that I surmised to be a backroom. Panic simmered in my gut. I'd wanted a little more time to look around before interacting with my employer. Maybe I could impress them with some questions based on my observations. A hand pushed the curtain aside. I was about to either get murdered and eaten, find out it was minimum wage with shitty hours, or meet some hulking, sweating thing I'd share a miniature cubicle with for a year. But it was only a small man—as weathered as the falcon gloves he wore—who stepped from behind the blind. The unsolicited email I'd received promised adventure, good pay, and the best company. The man in the falcon gloves (which by that I mean to say both of his arms, from hands to mid-bicep, were covered with thick leather) well, he didn't look like good company. In fact, displeasure shrouded his face. The canyon-deep lines of his skin suggested he wore the expression often.

He removed the gloves, exposing hairy arms crisscrossed with scars, which I hoped were from pre-falcon-gloved adventures of good pay. My mind jumped back to being murdered and eaten. The scars could be defense marks left by past "employees." My mother taught me to greet strangers, effectively stealing their mystery and removing their power.

"Hello, I'm Ale-"

"No need for introductions. I know everything and everyone coming through that door. Straight to business. While you're here, there are some rules."

Right. He was to stay in charge. "Rules. Okay, hit me." I regretted saying 'hit me.' First, it reeked of unprofessionalism and this was essentially a working interview, and second, axes, guns, and other obvious instruments of destruction littered the place. I shouldn't solicit physical assault.

The proprietor walked to the floor-to-ceiling windows at the front of the shop and picked up a spray bottle from a rust-covered cart. "Have you heard of The Poison Garden, at Alnwick?" He misted several potted plants, all larger than him as he spoke to me.

"No, I haven't."

"Well you needn't have, but this place is very much like that place. Just like the plants there, everything here will kill you. These plants, those dresses hanging near that deadly mirror, everything."

He gestured around the room with the spray bottle, which I feared would also kill me. I wanted to ask how a dress or mirror might end a life. The fabric of the dress, a dreadful grandmotherly floral couch print, was enough to induce vomit, but not an untimely demise.

"And I don't say that lightly," he continued. Rule number one: Don't touch a thing! Don't even think about touching things for some of the things here will know that you want to touch them and that is reason enough for them to kill you."

"Mr. Reaper-"

"It's pronounced Ree-pair it's french. But don't tell the customers that, it's better for business, more on brand, if they think I'm the soul collector himself."

I nearly scoffed. Apart from the scars and his controlling nature, he wasn't threatening. I regarded him only as a collector of lint from the bore hole of his belly button in the soft half globe resting on his belt. It was a stretch to envision others assuming him as Death.

"Is that rule number two? The not letting on about your name?"

"Ha!" he laughed, holding his ample gut as it jumped with each chuckle, most likely shaking the lint loose. "No, just a request. Rule number two is: Do not ask questions! My customers have very specific needs and death is a sensitive topic. I don't ask questions and so you shouldn't either."

I contemplated closing my eyes and keeping them shut, for the more I looked around, the more questions I had. What was the big, black box for? Who would ever need to purchase a two liter bottle of deadly nightshade? What did the partially wrapped (or was it partially unwrapped?) mummy winking at me know that I didn't?

"And this isn't like that bookstore...Mr. Penumbra's. I don't need you curious. No poking around. Don't open the books. Both curiosity and the books will absolutely kill you here."

I hadn't noticed the wall of bookcases framing

one side of the shop. Beyond papercuts and bonks on the head, how much damage could a volume do? Spell books would harm, if magic *was* real. Oh how I wanted to ask if magic was real, but determination to appear serious about my duties formed the words:"How will I know what people need?"

"Do not make suggestions. That is rule number three. The customers won't need help. Stay out of their way. Think of it as a self-service station." The giant plants now misted, Mr. Reaper moved to dusting. He pulled a large rag from his back pocket, gingerly touching the finishes of several objects, avoiding any moving parts.

"Do I need to take money?" As far as I could see, no deadly cash register sat on a front desk of any kind and no price tags hung from the items surrounding us. I imagined myself pricing everything with toe tags from a morgue, you know, to be more on brand.

"Finances are a private thing. Payment is made through the banks and pickup arranged according to each client's requests."

My heart sunk. I wouldn't be having any fun at this shop. It was a deadly serious business where humor had no home. My only hope of entertainment would be first time visitors. I could scare them, maybe play some pranks. People and cars hustled by outside. The shop sat on a busy street. Someone would fall into my playground. "What do I do if someone wanders in?"

He waved a hand in the air, dismissing the possibility. "No one wanders in. And if they happen to, they'll quickly wander out."

Well, fuck. I've had rough first days. There's

always a learning curve at a new job. In this case though, I wasn't even sure what I'd been hired for. Would I be the eventual gentle duster or monstrous plant mister? Maybe he had a second set of falcon gloves for me to assist with the beast in the backroom? The extensive collection of knives piled inside a display case behind me certainly looked in need of a good sharpening. "What can I do? Is there an employee manual somewhere I can read? Or a list of tasks?"

"Tasks will come later. For now, don't do anything. Just stand over there. Smile when the door opens, but don't smile too much. It may scare someone off." He pressed a stethoscope to the big, black box. I was no longer a smiling threat. What the hell was he listening to?

I stayed where I was. Honestly, relief surrounded me in my one spot. Fear filled me to the top that I might spring a trap if I turned the wrong corner. My lungs required convincing to inhale the potentially poisonous air. The email I received about the job said I should wear comfortable clothing. So here I stood in athletic pants (the tearaway kind with the snaps down the legs) a moisture-wicking shirt (which the mist-loving plants already had me grateful for,) and my best gym shoes. I'd assumed I'd be lifting and moving things, cleaning up, and restocking shelves. But standing around hardly seemed to require any kind of special, cozy clothes. If I was just going to stand there, give me a cool uniform like the possibly not empty suit of armor standing in the corner of the shop nearest the door.

□

I stood for a few hours, until my bladder screamed.

The bathroom was an actual closet without room enough to close the door unless one stood between the toilet and the wall. After gymnastic feats to maneuver in the coffin, I was grateful for my practical clothing. What would using the bathroom have been like if I'd donned the suit of armor?

When I was done, I saw that Mr. Reaper had strapped a gas mask to his face. He used a crusty funnel to refill the bottles in the glass cabinet. That was not a task I ever wanted. Not the poison refiller, not I. It seemed like a good moment to ask him about my hours. Not surprisingly, he had no idea.

"Unknown at this time," was what I think I heard him mumble through the rubber and filter on his face.

□

It was a busy shop. I practiced my partial, not-too-friendly smile on all sorts of shady customers. The suit of armor walked out the door with a man in a trenchcoat. Mr. Reaper brought out a covered cage barely holding something angry (he was wearing the falcon gloves again) and he handed it to a brute who had to stand outside because he couldn't fit through the door. Then, just before I thought my shift might be over, based on best guess and sun position, she came in.

A tall brunette of simple beauty. Porcelain skin, lips a natural, brilliant red. Her outfit screamed The Matrix. Her presence more commanding and assuring than anything I'd encountered so far that day, even the brute, because he was terrifying.

Mr. Reaper emerged from the back room before her beauty caused me to smile. "Ah, Ms. Jager. You arrived much sooner than I expected."

"I see my plants are doing well, Phillipe."

They are almost ready to eat people, I thought.

"Yes, splendidly. Thank you for the seeds. Are you well?"

"I am well, considering current affairs. That's enough pleasantries. You know I'm here for the child."

"We don't have any children here," I said to alert her to my presence and to assert my usefulness as a new employee, but then I wondered if maybe we did have a child here and I was unaware of he/she/it. Fuck, how hellish would this little thing be? Chucky scary? Children of the Damned disturbing? Maybe that's what was in the black box? Or perhaps the wretched thing was why he had to wear falcon gloves in the back room? Was 'child' a code word I hadn't been taught? It could be a derivative poison, or something for killing children. My imagination did me no favors. I didn't move from my spot. I smiled a little, but not too much. I didn't ask questions.

"Alexander, go with her," Mr. Reaper said to me without breaking eye contact with her.

She couldn't be talking about me, I hadn't been a child for almost fifteen years. "Sir, I don't know who she is. She said something about a child?" I watched his face for enlightenment, as though he'd suddenly recall some too-late-to-abort monstrosity hiding in a shadowy corner.

He chuckled. She tapped her foot impatiently. His cheeks flushed.

"I'm sorry, Regina. You must excuse this delay. It's always a hassle receiving these live shipments," he said to her and then turned to me. He whispered "child, your purpose is not here. It's out there with her."

"I'm not a child, I'm thirty-three. My purpose here is to earn a paycheck!"

"Yes, but she is over seven hundred, and I am just shy of that, which makes you a child in our eyes. But more importantly, you're deadly and that is why you are here and why you're leaving with Ms. Jager. The reward will be far greater than any paycheck. I'm sorry if that is too much to take in in one go or not nearly enough information at all, but her time is short and the world needs you and I'm not usually needing to convince the wares to leave the warehouse. She'll give you all the details." He stopped. I felt he had more to say, but he chose to take a few breaths instead.

He was right, it was a lot of information to process all at once, but my mind stuck to one concept. "I'm...deadly?" That was a question, shit. I turned to Mr. Reaper so it appeared to be directed at him and not Ms. Gorgeous-and-Named-After-an-Alcoholic-Beverage.

"In the right hands, absolutely. 100%! I can show you the receiving slip if you'd like. You're not an employee, you're inventory. Your ability to walk and open doors is what dropped you at the curb instead of my loading dock."

"But spiders frighten me. I only recently threw away my night light. How could I be deadly?" I didn't care who I was asking questions to then. Answers were required.

"I'll explain everything. Do not fear," Regina added, "we'll face no spiders or shadows."

Mr. Reaper laughed his belly-shaking guffaw.

I needed more than no arachnids and darkness. How could I leave on an unknown adventure with a complete stranger? "Whatever we're going to do together, will I die?"

"No, it's not possible, but you will kill many."

Not possible? "Will they deserve to die?"

A macabre smile bloomed on her face. "Oh, they have been asking for it for centuries. Now, get your things. I trust those are comfortable clothes as instructed? I'll tell you all about our quest on the ride to the manor. And if you have one of those smart phones, you can check your bank account. We've already deposited a first payment for your services."

I didn't want to leave the boutique, but I admit, I was intrigued. Beneath the sign, on the sidewalk outside the shop, I asked "how am I deadly?"

Ms. Jager, my new employer, stepped into the backseat of a waiting car and smiled up at me. "You are the perfect host, for your body is immune to all known disease. You've never been sick, but you can transport and infect. I have a strain of an ancient illness and a enemies who I've been unable to defeat until now. Get in."

I took a final look behind me, through the dewy glass and beyond the beckoning leaves of the maneaters growing there. Mr. Reaper waved to me with falcon-gloved hands. And just a little bit, not too much, he smiled.

STILL LIFE

My observations aren't paying off. Months have passed and I'm no closer to determining if I'm a vegetable in a hospital or a mummy in a museum. Is this mortal immobility or am I ancient immortal nobility? Dying or already dead? Doomed to waste away or preserved for all eternity?

The wall across the room holds art, but there's nothing notable on that canvas. Just a sad woman in pastels and heavy gowns. I can't turn my head to check the other walls. I feel a kinship with her. Stuck in one spot. Placed just so. Wrapped in bandages and cotton sheets or linen and resin. Sad and isolated.

I am clearly a spectacle, a specimen, a special case. Many people come by and visit, with mixed emotions. They hem and haw. Scrutinize. There is a lot of pointing in my direction, or maybe behind me, but I don't know what's there. Some of them cry. Many of them pray to God or gods. I haven't a clue the deity. I am breathtaking, but tragically or beautifully so? They leave flowers at my feet, out of obligation or in offering, I'm unable to surmise.

They talk to each other. They talk about me,

I believe, and maybe about what they should have for lunch after our time together. No one ever invites me for lunch. I'd like that.

Then there are those who clean me, dab lightly at the gauze covering my body, treat me delicately. I suppose I am delicate. But what are these wrappings for? Am I a broken body clinging to life or a dead one being held together?

There are others, the people in between. They come in and do things in the room, but never look my way. Shall I be thankful or offended or saddened that my charming, silent personality just isn't enough? My intrigue holds no power over them. They are the space cleaners, the trash takers, the general checkers of things, the guardians.

The lights go out every night, whether I'm ready to close my eyes or not. Or maybe my eyes are still open, but I can't sort that out in the pitch black. I can see small, multicolored lights dotting the room like constellations, from machines or security cameras or the backs of my eyelids.

Maybe it's enough that I know of museums and cameras and machines and lunch. That's my proof that I am a vegetable of this day and age and not a preserved corpse from another time. But I could have picked that up somehow or conjured the concepts to keep me company.

I can't feel my limbs. I can't speak. I've suffered some trauma to send me here, but here is far more traumatizing. My hearing is muffled. I'm underwater, effectively. Internal damage or decay? If I could only hear their words, I might sort my situation, determine my condition.

They've run scans and tests of all kinds, though I have no idea what they're looking for. They've constructed an enclosure around me. Is there something wrong with me or them? Who does it protect? I can see beyond it, and they, in. Something keeps me alive, perhaps an ancient magic or complex man-made machines. Some chemical elixir coursing through my veins or a natural solution conserving my tissues.

I'm sure I arrived with things, belongings, and they've taken them from me. Somewhere bagged and locked away or spiffed up and on display are my jeans or jewels, shoes or sandals, my barely theres or my burial wares.

□

For whatever reason, mine is an extended stay. I've now been here for so long, the painting has changed. The depressed woman now replaced with still life. A bowl of fruits. Perhaps to mock me, the vegetable, the mummy. I try to blink my eyes or the leathery skin around my sockets, once for yes and two for no. Just to let them know I am alive inside. But no one notices. No one ever sorts out the code.

Eventually I believe they'll come to collect me. Take me off of life support or the inventory list. Wheel me away on a gurney or handtruck. Pack me in a coffin or shipping crate, with silk or peanuts, to take me to another plane or another museum. A crematory or a conservatory perhaps. A hole in the ground or another tour around the world. I'll get visitors either way. At my grave or at my new exhibit. They'll leave flowers and only talk to each other. They'll talk about me, I believe, and about maybe what they should have for lunch after our time together. And they'll never invite me for lunch, even though I'd like that.

SKELETONS

do you like my skeletons?
you kept asking them to dance
often pulled them from their closet
in all their morbid elegance

'twas not enough to see their structure
'twas not enough to view their bones
you had to tap, and tug, and bend them
document each creak and moan

and when I told you that you knew them
assured you of your notes
you'd pull those monsters out again
to grimace and to gloat

'twas not enough to know them outside
'twas not enough to know them in
you had to pull each one apart
reconstruct each trial and sin

and now they stand between us
ivory relics, stiff as stone
and you cannot look around them
you only see me through their bone

do you like my skeletons?
I hope, for they live with you now
at your behest, at your commanding
cages you cannot disavow

THE CHIMERA PROJECT

She didn't know that suits came so pressed and fitted, yet there in front of her one clung to a man, barely allowing him breath and movement. His smile was as tight as his wear, and as cold and unexpected as the man himself. He carried no briefcase. She invited him in.

They sat across from each other. Each had a couch to themselves. But they, him out of business and his tight suit, and her out of nerves, occupied but fractions of cushions with their closed selves. She felt like he was going to tell her about a god or a vacuum cleaner. He wished he had something so wonderful and trustworthy to sell.

"You won't remember me. I'm certain there's no way you could. But I can still see the little girl I met so long ago."

She wasn't sure if there was emotion in his remembrance. He seemed to be merely stating a fact. "I have no idea who you are." There was no reason to play nice. She hadn't been expecting guests. Crumbs dotted the coffee table like seed spread for invisible birds. There were no clean mugs for tea. Even the dress she wore was in disrepair, it's zipper threatened to separate from the cloth it was meant to hold together. She grew self conscious of her hands and realized there was no proper place to put them. When she settled for her knees it made her look like she was either about to stand, just sitting down, or simply bracing herself for news of a terrible kind.

"I know this is awkward," he said, placing his hands on his knees as she had. Mimicry was a trick he'd learned to help others feel more comfortable. "There are only a few questions I have for you and then I can be on my way. I'll make this quick. And painless."

"Okay, go ahead." She waited for him to pull a notepad and pen from somewhere, as anyone interested in information might do, but his hands stayed on his knees.

"Growing up, would you say you had any trouble with that?" The man made a move to cross his legs, but his suit disallowed the position change. He rested his hands on either side of his legs, on the edge of the couch. Now he looked as though he was about to excuse himself to the restroom or to take a phone call outside.

She had a fear this man was exactly where anyone he knew expected him to be and so no interrupting phone calls would come through. Was he asking if growing up was difficult or if she had not wanted to grow up at all? She remembers feeling lonely, wishing she had siblings, and larger breasts. Her parents never had another child and when her breasts did come in, they still weren't to her liking. Otherwise, she always got what she wanted on her birthdays, dinner was ready every night at six o'clock sharp, and her parents had a wonderful collection of books they allowed her to read from. "My childhood was ordinary." It was all she could come up with to address the question. The man didn't need to know about her cup size.

"Ordinary, that's good. Did you deal with any health issues? Any pains or abnormalities?"

It was an odd question from a stranger, even from one claiming to know some past, adolescent version of her. There was the accident, one she remembered nothing about and was lucky to survive, so her parents and her scars told her. Otherwise, she got chicken pox with the rest of her class, her period the same year as her best friend, and her wisdom teeth taken out the day before her eighteenth birthday. "No. I grew up healthy. I get a physical once a year from my family doctor."

"Mr. Monroe, yes?"

"Yes...you know him?"

"I've worked with him in the past. About the same time you and I last met."

"How did you say that I know you?" She moved her hands to the edge of the couch, because she was about to run to the phone, or the front door, or the knife block. The man knew more about her than she knew about herself.

"I didn't. You let me in before I could explain myself. But, now that I have confirmation from you that everything is in working order, we can end this. No need for a re-introduction."

"End what?"

The man laughed a short explosion of disingenuous noise as stiff and emotionless as his smile and his suit. "Your purpose is obsolete. We've had unity for over thirty years now."

"I'm a human being. I have a life. You can't just end it. What do I have to do with unity?"

"You belong to the world, dear. I'll do what is necessary."

"You aren't making sense. I must ask you to leave." She started to stand, but he raised a hand to stop her.

"Look, I'm sorry. It was the wrong approach. I thought you'd know more than you do." He attempted to soften his face, but it appeared only as a collection of random twitches.

"What the hell is it that I don't know?"

"Tell me about your scars, Miranda."

She folded into herself once more, tighter this time. She tried so hard to hide them, the scar tissue that marked her abdomen and back, crossing like Nazca lines, with no known purpose. She was a victim and a survivor of something, but not even her mother would tell her what. "I've had them for as long as I can remember."

"The world hasn't always been a peaceful place. Back before you were born, as you were taught in school, wars raged between the three superpowers.

New battles began before old ones ended."

"But we signed a treaty and peace was restored. I know all this. I passed the history test."

"A treaty was signed, in the form of three orders for surgery. Of course this wasn't public knowledge because we needed to protect the anonymity of the families involved."

"Surgery?"

"Organ transplants specifically. Children representing each of the three countries received a gift from one another, a symbolic exchange of teamwork and cooperation. You are one third of The Chimera Project."

"I'm part of the Unification Act?"

"You *are* the Unification Act."

She thought of all the times her mother lied to her: when they shopped for beach suits and her first bra, at every doctor's appointment, and each time as a child her tub filled for a pre-bedtime bath.

"We easily could have kept you in a cage, dear, but we aren't inhumane. We couldn't tear apart families." Again he attempted a smile, but each effort was less successful than the last.

"You tore us apart! Children!"

"The three of you were a political statement. You were a peace treaty forged in flesh. Your parents volunteered you. You should be proud, like they are, to have served your country and the world."

"Proud? I didn't have a choice. And to think, my parents wouldn't let me get my ears pierced until I could fully understand the implications." She grabbed an earring as she remembered the conversation, which was a combined lecture on infection, reputation, and long-term commitment to scarring.

"So passionate, so lifelike." He raised a hand in caress, but the crumb-covered table offered the small comfort of slight distance.

"I'm not a fucking robot!"

"No, you're right. You do have the parts of a human." He pointed at her gut, where the traded organs resided.

She stood. "The parts? I have every human part! Get out of my fucking house!" She shouldn't have let him in. She shouldn't have let him stay. The hem of her dress hovered just above the table and somehow, with her knees sticking out, it made her feel more exposed.

"Calm yourself. Please, sit back down. Have you taken your packet of pills today?"

"You want me to calm down after telling me I have no claim to life and it's my time to die?" She estimated twenty steps to the front door and the path was clear. Her pills were digesting in her stomach, no longer "vitamins" to her, as her parents had called them. They were drugs to help avoid rejection of the transplants. She'd have to take them for the rest of her life, if she made it out of her living room alive. "What about the other two thirds of the project? Are they receiving similar visits?"

"If you knew me, you'd know I'm not usually this tan. I was in China just last week. I was unaware they had such beautiful beaches."

"So you've killed already." She took him in, gel-covered head to shiny leather toe. Indeed there were stark white slivers of pre-sun skin making occasional appearances when the sleeves of his suit jacket and button up shirt rose. Who wears a suit to the beach?

"I have...terminated the contracts, yes."

He was petite for a man, so frail and dry she imagined him as snappable as a winter twig. She could take him if necessary. Her dress certainly allowed greater movement than his suit. Or did they implant a chip in her heart set to explode on command? Where was the button? Would it hurt?

The man saw her thinking, working out an exit, an escape plan. He could take her if necessary. He was stronger than he looked and the fabric of his tailored suit was thirty percent of some stretchy material he could never remember the name of. Not enough stretch to cross his legs when seated on a couch. But more than enough to knock a leg or two from beneath a threat. As a last resort, he could punch her in the scar tissue on her belly. It worked on the European.

"I'm sorry, Miranda. We can't allow you to grow old. If you fall apart, if those organs fail, so does the treaty." The man drew a gun from his suit.

She had never seen such a low profile weapon.

He had never killed a woman before. His hand shook.

She was still trying to figure out where the gun came from in his restrictive wear as he pulled the trigger.

NOTHING IS PROMISED US, BUT DEATH

No one knew why the draugen emerged from the sea that day. We'd never seen them before; only heard they might exist, that they might pay our island a visit someday to wreak havoc on dry land. It may have been the death of Lev, when his fishing boat overturned, that tipped the scale. One body too many in that vast, watery grave, spilling the souls over the brim and back into our world. It must have been that, for they wore the faces of those we'd lost to the waves, to *Njörðr*, but their resemblance to our loved ones ended there.

A thick stench in the air preceded their arrival. The fishermen, haunters of the beaches and as old, crusty, and stuck to the docks as the barnacles, explained away the rank odor as an overabundance of algae. The rotting, briny scent clung to the hair in our noses, climbed down our throats, wove its meaty self in between every strand of hair and cloth on our bodies. We couldn't wash it out or off. Some claimed it hung so heavy it slowed the wind. There was an otherworldly, green hue to the usually invisible air.

The drugstore in town sold out of first aid masks, and bandanas, and rags, and anything remotely possible of filtering the saliferous, decaying reek before it hit our lungs. Not that any of it worked, maybe in a sugar-pill, placebo, hope-filled self-deception kind of way. The entirety of our fishing village looked like bandits, disguising our faces by partially obscuring them. Many of us developed an unfortunate cough, myself included. We lived like that, uncomfortable in our skin, for two weeks. Some left the island to live with relatives out of desperation to breathe normally again. But only a few, not enough to save lives, to really matter. Most of us were stuck there to suffer.

On the first day of the third week, Jul, the oldest fisherman on the island, with wrinkles deeper than the bay our community hugged, reported something strange he'd seen as he'd reeled in his fishing line. A thousand small domes, grey-black like the ocean that day, spaced equally apart, dotted the eerily calm sea. He hobbled up main street, his pole and bait box in hand, spouting a warning to anyone who'd listen. "It's them! The draugen have come to take us away!"

I'd never seen him so shaken. Jul helped raise me. I knew the man as well as I knew my own children and though he was on the verge of senility, I still found it easy to believe every word that crossed his permanently chapped lips. We all did. The older generations knew the lore, understood what was happening when the second phase of the attack began, when it could no longer be blamed on an unseasonably huge collection of miniscule organisms stinking up the place; what those grey domes on the water meant.

Our children had been spared the nightmares

through some unspoken, community-wide decision to omit the tale from story time. It was a narrative only told in bars at that point, not beds. A dying legend. We should have known that the undead didn't follow such rules, that no amount of omission would alter their existence or quell their anger. And at any moment, we'd have to let the children know the truth.

According to the stories, once the draugen heads appeared, there was nothing to be done to stop them. The draugen had formed their frontline. It was in our best interest to do the same. We stocked up on food and water and boarded our houses, always keeping one eye toward the water. The people here were rugged, used to a tough life in a harsh climate, but beyond a rare bar fight between drunken men, violence and conflict were uncommon. Being an island community of a peaceful country, few of us kept weapons. We raided our sheds-turned-armories for harpoons, axes, and hammers, fishing nets. Whatever we could find that might save us from that wet, horrible, approaching death.

One day was all we got to prepare for a war we didn't know how to wage. Like a marching army, the draugen moved forward uniformly, emerging from the water at a steady pace, their thousand undead bodies resolute against the retreating tide. The first row of draugrs reached the beach, their full grotesqueness exposed to air and eyes. Bloated, grey, and cumbersome now that they'd left their fluid home, their movements changed. They lurched and threw their arms forward and back in jolted mockery of living, breathing things.

They opened their mouths in unison, flashing gaping holes darker than the deepest depths from whence they came, darker than an impossibly starless night sky. A wail went up, that of foreboding, like a tsunami warning or a high-pitched foghorn. Very bad things were about to happen, it warned. The scream was a million voices pooled into one. It hit us like a shockwave, sending paralyzing tremors of pain and sorrow through our bodies.

As soon as we could move again, we didn't turn to flee. Those shambling relics of tragedies we thought we'd moved beyond, they held our gaze. Our feet sought to turn and save us, but our eyes refused to be torn from the occurrence. Like a harvest moon, huge and spectacularly-colored, or perhaps a migrating whale pod, the draugen were a sight to behold. Their skin was the dark grey of sand wet with water for building castles, with a hint of corpse blue throughout and as we watched them, they changed shape before our eyes, amorphous like jellyfish but as solid as the Lophelia reefs.

When Tore recognized his daughter, Astrid, who disappeared on the same beach last year after being stolen by the riptide while collecting shells, well... that was when we ran.

For two days, we hid in our homes while the draugrs roamed the streets of their former existence. From what I could tell, they were angry, but dumb. And though anger was enough to move their feet one in front of another, it wasn't much of a steering wheel. The large, storefront windows of half the shops on main street were decimated by reckless shoulders, and even one entire body, which tripped on the sidewalk and fell forward into the bakery's display case. Loaves of bread, cakes, and that thrashing draugr were all embedded with tiny pieces of glass. There was no word from the mainland; we had no idea if the draugen were endemic to us or if other parts of the country, maybe even the world, were experiencing the same thing.

Our houses were on a hill above the shops. The entire town was step laddered like that, with the bay, the beach, the business core, and the residential area all rising above each one before it. It took the entirety of those two days of dread for the draugen to climb the hill and reach our homes. And for the stumbling idiots that they were, more uncoordinated than our town drunks, they certainly seemed drawn to us, like sharks to blood.

They took the first of us in the dark, early morning of the third day of the third week. Hilde, the widow of Stig, found the man for which she still mourned. Or rather, he found her panties down while she was using the outhouse they'd finished building just before his passing. Her scream woke the rest of us, not that anyone was really sleeping with the beasts bumping against the weather beaten walls of our homes. We watched from our windows, robes pulled tight around our bodies. The full moon shone down on the scene like a spotlight, demanding we focus our attention on Hilde's slow, half-naked death. He gripped her by a wrist and dragged her quivering, blue-skinned body into the eventual darkness of the distance. Her shrieks began to blend with the howling wind until we could no longer discern the difference. If there were any doubts about their business on our island, they had been taken out to sea with Hilde.

In the later morning, when visibility was better, several fishermen led their families through the obstacle course of corpses, toward the docks and the boats that might save them. Draugrs pooled around the fleeing, undeterred by oars and broomsticks swung clumsily at them, and began to pluck the children out of the women's arms, like diving birds stealing fish from the sea. Those who reached the boats fared no better. Draugen still hiding below the surface flipped the boats and pulled them under, growing their future ranks with each drowning. We were powerless marine life stuck in our tide pool of an island.

I kept the children in their bedroom, near the center of the house in a way that dampened the terrible noises of the world as it was at that moment. They asked many questions, about their friends, about the animals left to fend for themselves, and about more trivial things like the ice cream counter in the store and the swings at the playground left unvisited and empty for the time being. We still coughed, but the sealed house did much to diminish the odor, as did the winter blankets held tight against our mouths to quiet the sound.

Jul came pounding on the back door one night, just as we were tucking into our cans of beans we jokingly called dinner. For a moment I was frightened to open the door even a crack, convinced that doing so would let a ray of life out like a lighthouse, sending signal to the undead drifters lost in the fog and guiding them to our shore. At a point I became more concerned with the noise Jul was making; surely that would lead them faster to us. I let him in and offered an unopened can to him, but he brushed it away with the same indifference he reserved for crabs and fish too small to keep. I imagined he would have tossed the thing if it had made it into his grip.

"I've come to ask for your help," he said. "I know you have the kiddies and you don't want to risk leaving 'em alone, but we're losing this battle. I've got a pile of harpoons and I need some men to wield 'em."

I could tell the dead had already touched him. He wasn't wearing a jacket--practically suicide at this hour and probably lost to grabbing hands--and bruises dotted his arms, overlapping the liver spots and coral and fishing scars in a grotesque, abstract pattern. His eyes told a similar story, frightened and red from crying over something so dreadful it shouldn't have been survived. He'd been there so much for me and after Else died, he was a substitute father as I grieved. But Jul, I just knew he wouldn't ask me to abandon my children if he'd been in a better state of mind. This was a man who looked like he needed a sedative and a walk back to his own bed. I couldn't provide him either, so I did the next best thing.

"You can stay here for the night or as long as you'd like," I suggested. "I can bunk with the kids and you can take my room. It's safe. We can make it through this together."

He hung his head, another gesture he repeated in the presence of wasted effort on the docks or out at sea. I was an undersized fish in his net, a loss to be thrown back and forgotten. He stood up and made to zip the coat he wasn't wearing. I pointed to the coat rack near the back door and he selected my best down jacket from its peg as though it was his own. He left, without a goodbye or a thank you. It was the last time I saw him.

Apart from what happened next, I do believe we survived as long as we did because we stayed low and hushed, hidden from the sea beasts and their inhuman hungers. The children were expert players of the quiet game and found a youthful enjoyment in creeping around the house, avoiding the windows and creaky floorboards.

On the night following Jul's strange visit, the nightmare found us. First, in my sleep. I was being followed by an animal. It was larger than I and larger than even it should have been and without seeing it, I could sense that. On the beach, I decided to turn and face it. A giant, earless, grey horse stamped its feet in preparation to charge. It turned in a circle and I glimpsed its full shape. The thing also had no tail and its back was broken so badly there was no way it was alive in the real sense of the word. Its mane, a tangled curtain of human hair. Again it stamped its feet and broke into a gallop toward me. As it grew closer I could smell the rot; I could hear pieces of its body falling off in reaction to the pounding of its hooves. Just as the revenant mount reached me, I was shocked awake by that sickly draugr scent, stronger than I'd ever smelled it before. It set off a coughing fit so violent, I was forced out of bed, into the cool morning airspace of my home, past the door to my children's' room, to take a lonely perch above the toilet bowl. I couldn't taste my vomit over the smell of draugen decay. Over the sounds my body was involuntarily making, I didn't hear the glass of the living room window break or the hooves clomping on the wood floor of the hallway.

And then that giant, undead horse was in the doorway morphing into the semblance of a crooked-backed man, his tangled beach hair sloughing off of his head. I'd seen them come out of the water. I knew how tall they were, but somehow this one, even with its broken back, now filled the bathroom doorframe, its shape still shifting even as I screamed. There was no way around his reeking bulk. Being this close to one of the draugrs, I heard a wet slithering from within, as though his body was but a putrid bag full of squirming eels, worms in people soup entangling themselves in constant search of nourishment.

He threw his body at me. I felt myself capsize, do a complete overturn, ending up face down on the bathroom floor. Hands grabbed my ankles. My lungs filled up, or at least it felt like they did, with water. I could taste the saltiness on my tongue, even through the draugrs thick stench. Ribbons of invisible seaweed and eelgrass wiggled across and wrapped around my limbs, a fear I remembered from swimming in dark waters as a child. I felt heavier than my one hundred and sixty pounds. I was waterlogged, becalmed, unable to move. My vision darkened as my soul was pulled into the abyss. The draugr, its clammy hands and dark, angry spirit, showed me how it feels to drown. I thought of the woman first dragged to sea. How, even before her body disappeared beneath the steel, liquid blue, she knew what was coming, could feel the saline pushing through her veins on overdrive. It's a horrific thing, to feel so full yet so empty at the same time, gasping and grasping, but to have nothing to grab hold of to save oneself.

Behind the brute, the children called to me. I could hear their small voices above the muffling water, testament to the decibel at which they shrieked; air forced from lungs and through miniature vocal cords as fast and loud as possible. "Daddy! Daddy!" A strange mix of excitement and fear, like opening a present and hoping for the best, while still preparing for the worst. It had been weeks since I'd heard them so thunderously and those were tones and temperaments usually saved for the first moments after a nightmare. But, I guess that entire experience with the draugen felt like the odd moment between sleep and awake, where nothing makes sense, when you're trying to determine what is real and what is a fata morgana on the ocean's horizon, a trick on the mind and eye. A mirage.

The thing in the doorway released its grip on me, turned and walked toward their room. The psychological water drained out of my body as swiftly as it had rushed in. I could move again. My nausea returned tenfold at the thought of the beast reaching them before I, Daddy!, could answer their summons.

I followed it and watched as another, smaller draugr blocked his path. The new one opened its mouth and I prepared for a horrible noise, but nothing escaped the void. It was instead what looked like a silent territorial pissing, a baring of teeth asserting dominance or dibs, or some other twisted claim of ownership over our home and those within. The display reminded me of the first wolves on a kill, pacing the perimeter in preemptive defense, wanting the still steaming blood for their own empty stomachs. Whatever it was, it worked. The first draugr retraced its awkward trail back through the house and outside to torment the unlucky inhabitants of another plot of land.

This is when the draugr still in my home, clearly female in a way I shudder to call delicate, noticed me. She moved snake-like in my direction, fluid in her motions. In command of the flesh she'd newly acquired for this visit, almost as though the body had been tailored to her soul. Unlike the others, who bore secondhand skinsuits of mismatched colors and shapes. Last year's trends, imports from the thrift shops of the mainland, children's self-selected, random outfits, bedazzled for no apparent reason with this and that from the ocean floor. No, she was different.

When I could see beyond the rot, for she was still falling apart like perfectly cooked meat, a graceful, putrid lamb chop, my heart sank. It was their mother, Else. The bearer of my babes who still called for me from their recently wetted beds. She'd followed the other draugr in through the front window. Maybe he was a companion, a sort of postmortem lover. The

103

love in my heart for her, and the fact that she'd made him leave, led me to believe it was only a coincidence. She'd already been looking for us, and he'd simply opened the door for her. Cleared a path, as it were.

I stood in shock as though the whole mass of the draugen were screaming again. She wasn't supposed to be here. It was true her body was in the sea somewhere, reduced to microscopic pieces by now, after having fed the fish for a time. But she didn't die by the water's cold embrace; her presence in that salty, slippery silk coffin was simply a burial. Else loved the waves and appreciated the ways in which they sustained the village she adored. Her final request was to be given to it, an offering of sorts, when her illness finally pushed her spirit from her body. It made sense then why she moved differently. Anger wasn't propelling her forward. She was no rudderless boat, resigned to travel wherever the ever shifting winds and waters took her. Else was the school of fish beneath the boat, there to keep the lonely traveler company, the glint on the crests of infant waves aspiring to reach greater heights but saving the dramatics for another day, the lifeboat on the horizon when dehydration and exposure threatened to steal a life too soon. She wasn't here to kill us.

My wife had taken advantage of the rise of the draugen to pay us a visit. As her reeking form drew closer to me, a flood of memories washed me away from the reality of the situation. I found myself wondering if she'd still be there in a week for our wedding anniversary. My heart grew full at the thought of showing her the children's newest artwork and how tall they'd managed to sprout in her time away. I stepped toward her, wanting the firmness of her hug around me and the smell of her golden hair filling my nose. The hiss, not her quick motion backward, was what stole the wind from the sails of my daydreaming. It wasn't a threat, but a reminder I think, that I wasn't able to touch her unless I wanted to drown. What she couldn't know was it killed me just as much to comply with the anti-contact. I was dying to hold her, to be held by her. But she loved me too much to allow me to love her. She was still one of them, brought back to life by the same dark magic as the others.

As she slinked toward the window, moving gently like an anemone in a soft current, I thought of her rising from the ocean. Her first steps on the seafloor as she approached land and the underwater climb to reach the beach. Was our town how she remembered it? Did her memories extend beyond us? Was the path simply one she'd taken too many times to count and, therefore, habitual? How well did she recognize our faces through the murk of the rotted, seafoamy vision she had to work with?

I boarded the window when the wind picked up, using its gusts to hide the hammering. Else stood watch over us, a silent, slimy sentinel. Her best qualities shone through her deadness. In life, my wife was attentive, dedicated, and selfless. No amount of time or tidal ebb and flow, no erosion of her physical being could kill those things in her soul. Day and night for a week, my beautiful—though fungus blooming—

partner kept the other draugen away. She was the only beacon of hope we had, our breakwater against the mega force that was this dead tide. As I sat inside listening to the dying screams of my neighbors, I, several times, started up off the couch to ask for her assistance in protecting more than just us, her earth and land bound family of three. But I knew she was already doing more than she should. If there would be hell to pay in the other world for her choosing to love instead of lay waste, Else would surely be made to pay it upon her return.

Fear bubbled up in me. Would those the draugen killed return from the sea at once? I looked for the faces of my neighbors in the mass of benthic bodies. We wouldn't survive if that type of endless cycle applied. I had only my assumptions and hopes that this unmappable event would peter out, would run its course. Thank god I was correct.

The evening before it ended, a stillness unlike anything I'd ever known settled over the town. There were no ripples on the surface, not even the birds sang. I nearly wished for the screaming of the gulls or the neighbors to start up again, then at least I'd know for sure we weren't alone. There was a palpable emptiness, a feelable finality, as though the bodies that were gone had displaced air in their presence, pushing it toward me, but now it had all rushed away to fill the voids, leaving us almost too free to move about. The beds of my children and I were the few warm ones left.

On the final day of their attack, when all destruction that could be done, was, I watched the draugrs wade back into the waves. Those that could, anyway. Some never made it to the beach, having decayed too quickly or been destroyed by someone's will to survive. Their corpses, with harpoons and sharpened broom handles protruding in all directions like sea urchin spines, rotted away on the sidewalks and in the yards. My wife, my incredible Else, was still on our deck, too weak to stand. I remembered her last words, from our wedding-bed-turned-deathbed: "Please, put me in the sea." It was a last wish I'd honor twice.

It was time to say goodbye, but even then she shied away from me. I picked her up and sucked in a huge gulp of air, a futile attempt to fight the rising waters inside my body. My gaze was skyward. That blue blanket mottled with white became my north star. As long as I beheld it, it gave my brain enough hope for me to continue breathing; that I was still above water, not sinking beneath it.

I struggled down the hill. Her greenish-grey skin had dried out and was cracking, resembling an emptied lakebed baked too long in the sun. It flaked away, like small sheets of seaweed. The others had rewetted themselves like sponges with each return trip to the sea, but she truly was a fish out of water. The breeze wasn't helping. It took pieces of her and whipped them around before dumping them into the waves. The ocean was calling her back and I wasn't moving quickly enough to fulfill the request.

Each step felt as though I was trying to run underwater. A fight, and a slow triumph every time a foot came forward. At some point, the children were beside me, cheering me on with a profound knowledge of all that had transpired and what needed to be done. That this time we could actually do something to save their mother. They giggled and pointed at my awkward gait. "Daddy, you lost your sea legs!" Their spirits were so incredibly unwavering, lasting like the marine paint on our boats. They bounced in my peripheral vision, buoys refusing to be swallowed by the chaos around them.

I collapsed on the beach, just short of the water, and rolled away from her. My body fell into what seemed like a natural depression, but my eyes took in the miserable sight of many similar troughs to our left and right. The rocky wakes marked death for many and stood out like repacked soil over refilled graves. There were bodies buried here, they voicelessly announced. What I first accepted as scattered driftwood, morphed as my vision focused further. Limbs littered the shoreline, pale and mangled into unplanned shapes. Eyeballs, their stringy muscles still attached, sat amongst the seashells and stones like the bulbs of minute bullwhip kelp, waiting for a playful foot to squish them. I imagined the sharp rocks digging into my neighbors' bodies, burrowing beneath the skin as hard razor clams into soft sand. Down the beach aways, my jacket clung to a large rock, soaking wet and partially shredded. Jul would have fought until he no longer could, be it with a halibut on the line, or against the mighty Krakenesque force of a draugr. He did not go silently into that final sleep; I was certain of it.

I accepted the sorrowful, rigid hug, grateful to be in control of its embrace. In the relative quietude, the deep, ragged inhalation of air into my lungs sounded mighty, the roar of a god standing atop the ruins of a battlefield, celebratory and exhausted. Above all else, just happy to be alive.

The tide was coming in and I sat with Else as it lapped at our toes, began to outline our thighs and encircle our waists. I was impervious to the cold, really it was nothing compared to what I'd felt as I'd held her. I considered going with her, lying down in the shallows and really feeling the drowning as I watched my north star grow dark and ever distant. Death in a way didn't seem so frightening now that I had tasted it. But I could hear those two earthly anchors behind me, my children, yelling, "Goodbye, Mother! It was nice to see you!" and I couldn't bear to add a second farewell to their words.

Many attended her first funeral, followed me down to the beach, watched me take a boat out with her body, held my children as they bid farewell to their mother from the safety of the shore. Now, we three stood alone as Else's body disappeared into the blue. I was soaked from my ribcage down and still seeking a natural rhythm of breathing. Our daughter spun a flower in her hands. One of the first to breach the soil and announce the coming spring. Our son, pointed to the ocean, farther out, where those gray domes once again dotted its surface. They began to sink, to lay themselves to rest once more. I'd never felt so happy to say goodbye to something.

On our way back up the hill, our son found a stick with which he poked the remaining draugr corpses. As our daughter hopped and skipped over those same stinking piles, she hummed a lullaby her mother used to sing to her. Because of Else, I knew they'd be okay. Always protecting them from the worst, if she could. A kiss on the cheek while covering a scrape so the blood wouldn't scare them into deeper pains. Thank you, my love.

No one knew why the draugen returned to the sea that day. We knew now of their existence; that they might someday return to wreak havoc on our island once more. Our loved ones newly lost would most likely be in their numbers, vengeful as the ones that took them. Us few survivors cautiously emerged from our shelters, bedraggled and stressed, starving and traumatized. Our lives now flotsam, floating wreckage, proof of the storm. The children knew everything now and the tale of the draugen was no longer folklore, it was history. Written into textbooks and commiserated over at the bar. I was pleased to find out that both the schoolteacher and barman had survived, necessary for the healing distraction my children and I, respectively, needed.

The noxious smell lifted after two days. We cleaned up, collecting the pieces of our lives and our dead like seashells and beach glass, with reverence and attempts to identify the shards. With dynamite we blew holes in the island to build precautionary shelters, we questioned every smell wafting inland, and we went on living, albeit with skepticism, until the next onslaught, until the sea sought to take us again. I spent many hours, when the water and world were calm enough, looking for the significance of it all, a solid lesson I could take away to give meaning to the suffering. All I could come up with was that we have finite existences, like tiny, fragile boats bobbing along on the unpredictable waters of life. Carried only by the hope, but no guarantee, that we'll keep afloat to see the next sunrise.

It's up to us to make what we can of the sailing, for nothing is promised us, but death.

Michelle von Eschen

THE ANNIVERSARY GIFT

I was never one for picking gifts. Holidays and birthdays were unwanted opportunities for me to disappoint the ones I love, to remind them I hadn't been listening all year at the dropped hints, that not one ounce of creativity hid in my brain. After a few sorry occasions, I'd switched to gift cards, but even those were met with disdain. "Too impersonal," my wife had called them, even after gifting dish towels herself. I had a knack, too, for buying gift cards for the wrong places, but how was I to know my mother-in-law didn't frequent the hardware store? Didn't all homeowners?

Anyway, at least with wedding anniversaries, there was a guide. An elemental table of love, if you will. The list reeked of tradition, something my wife loved, and it remained my go-to for the last nineteen years. I blindly followed it, giving her presents of wood, silk, and lace on the corresponding anniversaries. China would be easy this year, but my wife deserved something more than fancy dishes. And knowing myself, I'd choose the wrong set. We'd sit for countless dinner parties, slowly uncovering the ugly design, staring as it stared back at us, daring us to replace it. But you can't

113

throw out that stuff, not when it was an anniversary gift. We'd be stuck in an unhappy, loveless affair with the painted plates and gaudy gravy dish, feigning agreement when the guests inevitably compliment it. So china simply—complicatedly—would not do. This beautiful woman, who moved with me and a job offer to the frigid asshole that is Minnesota, who gave up her warm, charming home, her happiness, and excessive amounts of vitamin D in south Florida to continue to choose me every day, she required the most unique of gifts. Something as one-of-a-kind as her.

□

It was over our morning breakfast, just after she declared "you've brewed the coffee perfectly!" that the idea struck me. Turns out there was an ounce of something creative in my brain, at least nine ounces if you counted the pot of perfection I'd made. Instead of boring, poorly-chosen china, I'd give her the gift of a dinner instead. I know, it sounds like an average anniversary, the thing all couples do, but I would make the dinner an experience. I—who really was nothing more than a button-pressing king of convenience, skilled at reading box instructions and leaving the heavy lifting to the microwave—I would cook the dinner myself.

□

Sourcing the ingredients was an adventure, one that took me all over the city to the overpriced artisan markets and hole-in-the-wall restaurant-slash-stores-slash-circle jerks owned by young, cocky, heavily-tattooed chefs. The ones who made love to food with their eyes and knew how to butcher animals into all their usable parts. The ones whose greatest aspiration was to get a cookbook with their name on it, but who would settle for street cred, pussy, and the occasional article proclaiming their culinary genius.

The potatoes and herbs for a mash were harvested fresh from the ground and blessed between meditation sessions by inner city monks. I pictured the fenced in garden, fed by dirty rain and patrolled by greedy pigeons and a cat named something inappropriate like Ahimsa, because the kill count of that shedding menace would top the mobsters of surrounding blocks.

The wine I discovered covered in dust at the back of a bookstore that used to be a bar, and I paid a hefty price for its vintage, mashed from grapes sometime just after the dawn of man. The label, an indecipherable scrawl, didn't have to be read to know the content was worthy of the predictably clever name. It "pairs well with red meats," the bookseller-sommelier told me without solicitation. The bookstore wine cellar definitely had a cat. His name was Hemingway or Merlot, I'm confident, even though I forgot to ask, because some things are just predictable like that.

I needed a vegetable and ended up with some mutant, hybrid thing from the farmers market. It was tomato mixed with ego, really. It should have been labeled "look what I can do." I just hoped it had taste to match its pretentiousness. Sometimes quality gets dropped in the creative process, like a garment made hastily for the runway that falls apart after that single walk.

The protein was most difficult to procure, though it shouldn't have been. We're surrounded by butcheries of varying specialties. I had my choice of meats and my wife is a true foodie who'll eat anything. She isn't even grossed out when Andrew Zimmern eats grubs and spiders and shit. I needed to wow her and New York was a melting pot of cultures for me to draw from. But what delicacy would impress her most? It all seemed overly mundane.

I'd been slowly convincing myself I could do it since just after our anniversary last year. The city was a crazy place, but no where that I knew of was it kosher to waltz in requesting a prime cut of human being.

There was a Japanese man who had eaten a woman and become famous for it. Of course he killed and devoured the nice girl in another country, and somehow all was forgiven in his homeland. He went on to write a book or two on the event, including details of the murder and the days that followed. People paid to eat beside him. My wife and I cringed, but then quickly dove into a serious discussion on the consumption of human flesh. The pros and cons of the task. I was on the fence, but would have tried it had it been given to me. My wife had no qualms. Absolutely none. That Japanese man became famous for it. I, well, I only needed my wife to know how much I loved her.

It would have been nice for us to choose the main course together, like a couple selecting their wedding cake, considering different combinations and dissecting layers, touching on the merits of each. But the steps following the selection would be gruesome and I knew she'd insist on helping if I let her in on my plan. So I kept it a secret. I told her I was taking a business trip, but instead rented a motel room above the dirtiest corner in the city and spent almost a week watching the human trash get taken in and out by only slightly less dirty humans. She couldn't be a hooker or a druggie. I wouldn't risk hurting my wife. I needed a homeless, helpless, lonely girl who'd do anything for a meal. New to the streets and not yet desperate enough to have turned any type of trick for survival.

She was a young Marilyn Monroe, ethereal blond and adequately curvy, but still not fully aware of the power of her beauty. I didn't ask her name, assuming she'd lie about it anyway. She sat on the edge of the queen bed, her outfit—a bold collection of all neons—enhanced the fade of the overwashed comforter beneath her. She chose the corner closest to the door. It was smart in a sad way and most likely a habit born from a bad past experience. At least when this bad experience was over, she wouldn't be living with the memories.

"You can relax," I said, my own voice rippling from nerves.

"Have you done this before?" She struggled for a moment with the zipper on a tiny purse she held and removed a condom once she'd gained access.

"No!" I replied too rushed and angrily as though she knew exactly what "this" was. No, no I haven't lured a young woman to her death for human consumption. First time for me. I usually stick to the anniversary list.

The takeout food sweat circles of condensation onto the chipped formica table. I pulled the table away from the wall, fearful the rising heat might encourage the already sagging wallpaper to slough off completely. I'd ordered from an Italian place because they'd bring wine. The drug mixed easily into the white. I'm ashamed to say I know a guy who got me what I needed under the promise of anonymity I required.

"Come eat, have some wine."

"You don't want to fuck?" The word never sounded so harsh as when it shot through her lips.

"That's not my interest. I invited you for dinner." Truth be told, I could have had her. No one would ever be wiser. But that would be like dropping the meat on the floor and picking it up to still serve it. That, and I loved my wife. I wasn't doing this for a thrill. There was absolutely nothing fun about planning and executing a murder.

"So...you like dudes or what?" She hugged her body and I knew my denial of her stoked the fires of a baseless insecurity many youth can't seem to put out.

"No, nothing like that. I'm married. But I'm here on business and I'd like some company. You looked hungry and I ordered for two. Force of habit."

She hopped off the bed and sat across from me. "Are you gonna drill into my head or some fucked up shit?"

"What?" My surprise was genuine, but not for the reasons she hoped. I was curious about a nibble or two of her brain. Plunging a drill bit into it seemed like a good way to ruin the tissue.

The guise of age her makeup gave her disappeared under the tube lighting mounted above the table. She was less a Marilyn and more a heavier set daughter of The Brady Bunch. Once she was close enough to the food to smell it, she greedily dug in. The first glass of wine disappeared. I was pouring the second when she closed her eyes and slid from her chair. I laid her on the bed, taped her wrists and ankles together, wrapped my belt around her neck, taped pillows around her head, laid on her body and pulled tight. She smelled like rain on concrete, and cigarettes, with hints of roasted garlic when she exhaled. My weight was enough to keep her thrashing to an acceptable, sellable, sex-related minimum if any neighbors were to hear. She went as quickly as her meal had. Now, the real work began.

□

The rings of the shower curtain dragged slowly across the rusted rod, as resistant as the girl's dead weight on the motel room's matted and stained carpet. I expected cumbersome, but this was a joke. At least my saw blade was sharp.

I'd read up on dismemberment, but nothing prepared me for the reality of it. Several times I wanted to give up, but my wife deserved this and I couldn't waste the body. I threw a washcloth over her face, envisioned a large chicken or pig, both of which I had seen butchered on t.v. and in online tutorials, and hunkered down. I found where the joints connected, used them as my guides, let the body do the work. It got easier, I found my flow. I packaged up the pieces I'd be cooking for our meal, and stacked them neatly in a duffle bag, surrounded by ice packs for the drive home. Her back fat, skin, and blood would be the start of an amazing black pudding. Recalling episodes of Dexter and CSI and SVU and every other homicide show I'd ever seen, I cleaned the bathroom meticulously with the chemical contents of overpriced, travel-sized, dust-covered bottles plucked from the stuffed shelves of a mini mart.

□

I expected regret to join me tubside, as her blood raced down the drain, but my smug solitude remained uninterrupted. Pride pulsed through me. I'd done the hardest part, assuming I had the marinades and cook times correct. Really, it wasn't even the worst this bathroom had seen. I could tell by the grime-covered grout separating the dated, pastel blue tiles, and the poorly patched cracks in the vanity mirror; I was not the first. I did not christen this ceramic with a broken body. She was not the only person to end up in pieces in this place.

□

I was only a man on a business trip and running household errands, if you followed my receipts or my tracks. The hacksaw I'd paid for in cash from a cut-it-yourself Christmas tree farm. I felled a small tree and survived a "you're no man at all" staredown full of judgment from the owner of the property. But maybe I live in a studio apartment that is basically one room with a toilet behind a flimsy partition and the tiniest mature tree ever known to mankind was all that could fit near the heat register without going up in flames due to proximity. The tree was dying on the side of the road where I left it just after purchase and I'd chucked the saw over a barbed wire topped fence into a junkyard pile where it would fit right in with its metal friends. Her clothes went into a black garbage bag with some random pieces I'd purchased from a second hand store. That medium lump of coal got slung into a turquoise donation bin in the parking lot of another convenience store. Nothing to see here. Maybe just a man making space in the second bedroom closet after his teen daughter has gone off to college. And in the great circle of life that is reduce, reuse, recycle, they'd end up back where half of them came from and I'd cause déjà vu in an underpaid, shady as hell part-time employee.

The rest of the pieces went into plastic bags and then a metal suitcase. I hid my phone deep in the old couch hugging one of the dirty walls of the motel's small lobby. There was no way I was going to let it ping to cell towers on my drive to the woods where I buried the suitcase. I returned for it early the next morning, claiming it had simply fallen from my pocket while I sat a moment.

□

I returned beaming and triumphant to our home, clutching bags full of ingredients in my arms like an Oscar collection.

"How was your trip?" my wife asked as she snooped in the bags.

"It was meh. I'm just happy to be home with you." I poured her a glass of wine, a red blend to which she was hopelessly addicted, and pushed her from the kitchen.

She poked her head back in the doorway leading to the living room and frowned. "I love watching you cook, honey, you rarely ever do. Let me stay?"

"I insist you leave. It'll ruin the surprise and you make me nervous." I needed time alone with the fruits of my labors.

☐

Soon after, my wife's laughter bubbled in from the living room as water boiled on the stove for the monk-blessed potatoes; a duet that temporarily calmed the trepidation I felt for having brought evidence of my crime into our home. This poor girl's dna would mingle with the already wilting mint sprigs abandoned on the counter from my wife's midday homemade mojito— an anniversary tradition—and bump shoulders with the bread crumbs overflowing from the catch beneath the toaster-a fire hazard we ignored. Suddenly our pre-fab, poorly planned kitchen was too humble, not fit for entertaining even the entrails of this beautiful girl whose life had ended for our enjoyment. A gourmet kitchen might be suitable to honor her sacrifice. Her dark, cherry red muscles deserved to rest on the rock greys of a pricey marble slab like the offerings they were.

Our kitchen island was tiled in once-upon-a-time white. I imagined the grout holding more microscopic scraps and secrets than the blue tile walls surrounding the motel tub. It was a two-and-a-half foot by four-foot block of foodborne illness waiting to happen. I pulled butcher-paper-wrapped cuts from one of the bags and prepared to face my deed again.

The noise of the salt grinder brought me back to the tub, where a hacksaw worked at bone with similar grating persistence. Both caused me to sweat. I rubbed the white granules into her meat, a post-mortem massage I found slightly erotic. It was then that my wife came in to refill her wine and wrap her arms around me, dangerously close to my filling erection.

"Oooh, that looks amazing! Where did you get it?" She flipped over the butcher paper to answer her own question, but it bore no logos taking ownership of the meat in front of me. I'd purchased the thick, brown wrapping and some string from a restaurant and kitchen supply store to keep up appearances, but I never expected she'd ask. One of the best things about special events in a couple's life: you are allowed to keep secrets in the name of the occasion. "That's part of the surprise, babe. Now let me get back to work so we can enjoy it."

"Okay, all right. But you know that can't be nuked, right?"

I laughed. "The oven is just like a big microwave. At least that's what I'm telling myself."

□

The genetic mutant of a tomato I'd found sliced clean and wet, yielding itself to the blade as though it were born to be sectioned and consumed. Could you breed a more sliceable tomato? I suppose a firm skin helps, but ripeness also alters the results. I drove the knife through the holy potatoes like a crucifixion, merciless and messy and then further tortured their parts with a masher. As I squished the living hell out of them, the motion reminded me of the mortar and pestle my friend used to crush the girl-numbing pills into a white-wine-fine powder. God, had I really done this?

I seared, I baked, I simmered. I used appliances and contraptions in our kitchen whose existence prior had been unknown to me. Our regular, old plates would have to do, just as the kitchen had. And then, the anniversary gift was ready.

Her favorite wine had done major work. She was all smiles as she sat before the buffet. Nerves caused my hands to tremble, sending my fork and knife clattering against the edges of my plate. It was an unintentional drumroll, a signaling for a toast I didn't know how to make. This would be the ultimate expression of dedication to our union. I mean, you can't part ways after consuming another human together. This meal, this death, would bind us for life.

"My dearest love," I began, "tonight we celebrate our anniversary. And I've prepared for you a unique feast which I hope will meet your culinary expectations. I couldn't buy ugly china, I know you'll understand. Happy Anniversary, babe." I beamed as wide as she. I raised my glass and as it kissed hers, I began to fret over our next anniversary. How would I ever be able to top this one?

She laughed. "It smells amazing! Happy anniversary. Thank you for coming home in time to celebrate."

I lifted the metal cloches. Human prepared properly doesn't look human at all. Her eyes sparkled, she licked her lips. "It all looks perfect, honey, and you didn't burn anything!"

I forgot to mention that I usually do burn the meat if I end up charged with its preparation. But I had more reverence for these cuts. I knew them personally. I sat with them for dinner. Though I'd only spent just under a half hour with her alive, this vagrant was to me a hog raised from piglet. A pride. I should have asked for her name, but Marilyn seemed so fitting.

My wife was savoring her first piece, something fatty from the thigh I believe. I watched her masticate the young girl and I recalled how the dinner ate her dinner in the motel room. The opposite of this. Ravenous and desperate, without regard for heat or flavor. Where she had spent seconds, my wife took two minutes at minimum.

"It's different, but I can't figure out how. Will you tell me what it is?"

"Have some more. Try a piece from this platter." God, I was enjoying it. I had some myself and I have to say I was impressed with my pairings of sauces to flesh. Urges to relate the pains I went to in order to provide the meal were overwhelming. I was desperate to impress her with descriptions of the river of hipsters I'd waded through to bring her this specialty meal. And, of course, I was itching to drop the bombshell of the most secret ingredient.

We ate together and reminisced about our years and adventures. I watched her tug on an earlobe as she spoke, something she'd done since before we met. Our feet waltz beneath the table.

When her stomach was begging her to stop filling it, she ran her tongue over a rib bone, dropped it atop the pile she'd built on her plate, and smiled at me. It was a grin of pure content, a "you've done well" showing of teeth. Her hand reached across the table and held mine. Another smile, this one more sinister, broke and spilled over the last. "Darling, she was absolutely delicious!"

"How did you figure it out?" I admit I was saddened that she'd stolen the opportunity for my grand reveal, but at least she wasn't disturbed.

"The shape of the ribs and you left a bit of skin on the thigh. It had a birthmark." She held up the small swatch of flesh. How could I have missed it?

"And how did you know it was a woman?"

"They are easier to kill, I imagine. Am I right?"

She was. "It was easier than picking the right China. That's for fucking sure."

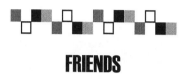

FRIENDS

"They say, they say I shouldn't talk to you," he admits, head hovering over his cereal like a storm cloud, but I understand he's addressing me and not the soggy flakes swimming in that white, shadowed lake below him.

"Tyler, they don't get to decide things like that." I'm leaning against the counter, ignoring the clock that ticks ever closer toward late-for-school-and-work-o'clock. This conversation is long overdue. He's been on about "them" ever since he could talk. From what he's willing to tell me, which isn't much, I know it's a boy and a girl. For imaginary friends, they don't seem like much fun. I thought they'd go away as he got older, but that day hasn't come. I could take him to get evaluated, but fear of what the psychiatrists would tell me about his development keeps me from such prying measures. Everytime he talks about them, I have this horrible habit of looking around as though I'll catch a glimpse. His confidence in their existence makes them feel real to me. At least as real as ghosts who simply choose to stay hidden from sight. Ones who disappear as soon as they enter my field of vision.

I've been thinking of ways to wean him off

them. He talks to them more than me some days. Attempts to get him to leave the house with me are futile. He doesn't want to be seen with me and that I get. Today, he crosses over to teenhood. His friends will matter more. Not dear old dad, not anymore. From here on out he'll ask for money and an extra hour or two before curfew. He'll no longer ask me to play catch in the yard.

It was better when he couldn't talk. When he'd just look at me and smile, follow me around, not question my authority. I guess all kids are like that, more defiant as they grow up. It has always been the two of us and I wonder if that's the cause of some of his trouble. Maybe I'm not enough, so he supplements with the imaginaries. His mom has been gone so long, I barely remember what it was like having her around. She is old wallpaper, forgotten beneath new layers of life.

He slurps milk from his spoon and it dribbles down his chin. "They say that smoking is bad for you. You should stop."

I take the millionth drag from the hundred thousandth cigarette. I picture them holding their noses, showing him pictures of cancer survivors and those not so lucky. But I remind myself he has made them up, and their imaginations are only as creative as his. "How do they know I smoke, Tyler?"

"I told them." He dumps spoonfuls of milk onto the remaining bits of cereal disintegrating before him. I relate too easily to the drowning victims, as powerful forces they have no hope of prevailing against are heaped upon them. When did my son become a sell out?

I flick the ashes into the ceramic ashtray on the kitchen counter. You know you have a problem when your kid makes a bowl meant for fruit in art class and you repurpose the ugly, lopsided thing into a receptacle for cigarette butts. It's true, I should stop. I've always felt guilty for smoking around him. When he was younger, he thought the "clouds" were cute. He'd dance around in them, looking for shapes as though he were peering at the sky. But it's really starting to piss me off that he's telling them shit about me. Jesus, I'm talking like they exist again. He could be using them to voice his opinions and that's actually kind of a healthy thing. Other parents have to desperately yank communication out of their kids. Not me, not me. Mine just spews it.

"They want you to go away."

These words threaten to haunt me. I expect they'll take acts against my life next, muster all the cosmic forces to leave a scratch on my arm or something. Falling asleep from here on out will be a russian roulette. Any night could be the loaded chamber, the night from which I don't wake up because the spirits of his adolescence have come for me.

"Well I want them to go away! How does that make them feel?" I burn through the rest of my cigarette in one long, anxiety-amplified drag.

"I wish you would just leave me alone!" He dumps the remaining cereal into the wrong side of the sink, the one without the disposal. Someone will have to fish out the clumps of bran blocking the drain. Someone means me.

"And just what would you do without me?"

"I don't know, but I'll figure it out." He shrugs too easily.

That one hurts. He'll figure it out; like I figured out how to raise a child on my own. Like I figured out how to be enough for someone, which I apparently haven't figured out at all. For now I'm going to blame it on the hormones. He's growing up too fast. I am a bird watching it's fledgling jump from the nest for that first flight. I'm losing my grasp on him. He spreads his wings and flees the kitchen. I dart after him, but he's young and quick. Did I mention it's his thirteenth birthday? The clock hits his birth hour and minute, 8:02. "Happy birthday! You're late for school!"

There are days when parenting doesn't go as planned, like a cake mix in which you've dropped too much flour. You add more water and knead the hell out of it expecting to get the same workable mass the recipe instructs should come of the effort, but it only makes it worse. Nothing you do can salvage the cake, or the day, even if it's only 8 am. I refuse to call it a wash, scrape the ruined batter into the trash by breathing deeply and collecting myself, and try to turn the knob of his closed bedroom door.

He has locked me out of his room. A force pushes me aside and I look to my right where the hall should only be haunted by memories. There, two people begin to fade into view. Like a dimmer switch slowly lifting, they appear before me. At first I can see through them, but now they are filling in. Their voices started as distant too, muffled, like listening from underwater. Now they're screaming so loud I'd like to dip beneath the surface again for some respite. For a long time I've wanted this, to see them. But fuck, it's terrifying. I'm going fucking crazy. He even kicked the imaginaries out and now we're all standing in the hall, yelling his name.

They're much older than I imagined. They look more like him than I do. No wonder he feels closer to them. I let out a cry, mourning the similarities I lack. I could be a distant cousin, a neighbor, a fellow countryman. They couldn't care less for me as their fists fall heavy on his door. Their love for him overwhelms the hallway, building up into a fourth entity standing beside us. The door must open, I feel that urgency. I raise a hand to join them in their pleas, but my hand isn't there like it used to be. I can see through it. Somehow my own light is dimming. I ache to run to the kitchen, where I last remember being whole, but I can't leave him. Nonetheless, I feel far from him. Like he has forgotten my name and somehow I know he won't ever call it again. And I know, I know it was me the whole time. I was the made up thing, the pest, the imaginary. They get to have him and I don't.

I focus hard, reaching into the nothing for the dark energy that will allow me a moment extra. One more day with him, one more cigarette, one more chance to make the batter right. Maybe I can take him with me, wherever I'm going, but the door and his maturity deny me such a pleasant ending.

My sudden obsolescence reminds me of his teddy bear, dragged everywhere for years, worn to rags and missing an eyeball. He lives in a trunk in the attic. Am I going to some storage facility for unwanted friends? Where am I going? Where in the hell am I going? Do I get another chil—

VADLEÁNY

The tavern door burst inward and the heat and drunken happiness of the room left at once. A muscular, snow-covered man crossed the threshold and collapsed to his knees. He began to sob as the wind pushed dancing tendrils of white across the floor around him. No one rushed to his side. Instead, they bowed their heads as though praying to the drinks before them, too aware of what his agony meant. *She* had taken another.

Etil, the village cobbler, drank only water in his usual seat, a dusty corner far from the usual raucous patrons that dominated the barstools. He knew every pair of feet in the tavern and the people carried around by them. The man on the floor at the door was József, the town blacksmith, recently returned from a supply trip to another village. His wife Erzsébet, heavy with child, had gone with him, but by the looks of it, had not come back. Technically, *she* had taken two.

She was Vadleány. The wild woman of the woods. The devourer of man. According to the stories Etil had heard since he was young, she would appear before those traveling through the woods, naked and in need. What Vadleány needed would change depending on whom was standing in front of her. Somehow the girl knew each villager's sensitivities and vulnerabilities. Her long hair would be parted down the back and brought over her petite shoulders to cover her breasts and the delicate space between her legs. She never spoke a word, instead appealing to the hearts of her victims in a mysterious, silent way. She had emptied many a bed, ended entire bloodlines one by one, all to satiate her appetite for flesh. Fear of Vadleány was so strong that no villager was allowed to wear their hair longer than their shoulders.

In the tavern, the extra chairs had been removed and stored away, unwelcome reminders of how many, how much, the feral woman had taken from the village. Etil imagined them deconstructed and reconfigured, the legs crossed and shaped into grave markers. A cross for every life gone. Now, the barmaid rushed to make another disappear. The void of space above it wouldn't help the returned blacksmith with his troubles. Someone would quietly sneak from the bar while he drank away the memory; they'd walk to his home through the snow, hide the baby clothes and crib, his Erzsébet's dresses, her craftwork. When dawn broke the next day, life would have already seeped in to fill the cracks and holes left by this, the most recent disappearance. They'd all force smiles and continue on as though the wretched night before hadn't happened. But the village grew quieter and quieter.

Etil felt great sadness over the most recent loss. He was close to the blacksmith, as his tools and the nails he used came from József's shop. He'd allowed

Etil into his workshop to oversee their production. The clanking of the hammer on steel was a sound bore into his mind, one he'd never forget, and a noise that made him grateful for his much quieter profession. The baby was expected to come soon. At one time the men had laughed about József's giant, rugged hands, and if they would be capable of holding something so delicate. Etil was making a pair of booties for the child, but now, the shoes would sit on the shelf for the arrival of a someone else's progeny.

"We heard the leaves!" the mourning blacksmith yelled after drinking an on-the-house mug of ale in one giant gulp. "We waited until it was safe to pass, but she still came and took them!"

The woman in the woods never attacked after she'd eaten. And the leaves always rustled as she slept and digested her taking. If the blacksmith heard the leaves then why were his wife and unborn child ripped from his life by Vadleány's hunger? Etil had yet to be terrorized by her presence, having always taken advantage of those rustling leaves to travel the path to the next village. The woods were normally still, but a winter storm shook the small village and its surrounds. Maybe the man and his lover were tricked by the wind and it wasn't safe to pass when they did? It didn't matter now. It couldn't be undone.

Murmurs of discussion, speculation on what that could mean, broke out across the room. Long ago they stopped seriously planning the wild woman's hunt and slaughter. She was stealth, smart, uncatchable. Like a squirrel or bird, always on high alert for dangers around her, Vadleány never stayed in one place for any period of time. No one even knew her true age.

Etil closed his eyes and listened to the tavern. The blacksmith sobbed, glasses clinked as they met accidentally, for no one was cheering anything tonight, stool and chair legs scraped against the wood floor, libations were steadily poured as round after round was requested. He'd had a love affair with alcohol once, but it became an obsession leading to injuries in his workshop and a drop of quality in his work. Wasted leather meant more trips through the woods. Still he enjoyed the atmosphere of the bar. It was the one place everyone congregated, the sounds comforted him almost as much as the alcohol had, and they knew not to serve him anything other than water.

Hours later, most of the village had left for the night, save for a few of the most drunk, the mourning blacksmith included. "I got an arrow into the creature," he muttered. "Heard her yelp, like a wounded animal." Alcohol always made men boasters and liars.

After leaving the tavern himself, a sense of dread overcame Etil. His leather supply was nearly depleted as he'd already put off a trip to replenish it. At one time, he could locally source the required material for his work, but the tannery owner had fallen victim to the wild woman a few months prior and the man's apprentice had yet to produce anything usable. If he left in the morning, perhaps Vadleány would still be slumbering. He could travel quickly and make it back through the dangerous wood before she awoke.

The next day, he stood at the edge of the

western wood and listened for the leaves, but heard only a distant bird calling out and perhaps announcing his presence; the stillness a sharp contrast to his quickening pulse. Most likely, she was watching him, watching the vein in his neck dance as his heart began to fret over its fate. He couldn't stand there for much longer. The cold was tightening its grip and she would do the same if offered the chance. Turn around, do not enter, do not *die*, his mind screamed at him to choose other than what he was about to do. Etil looked down at his shoes, one of the first pairs he'd ever made. They too chose to walk forward. After an hours journey, when he knew he was nearing the other side of the greenbelt, he saw something ahead.

In the distance, an unnatural, lightly-colored heap sat square in the center of the path. Etil walked slowly toward it. Rising up from its middle, a narrow shaft pointed to the sky. The blacksmith's words echoed back in his mind and Etil knew that the man wasn't rambling, that the alcohol was telling the truth. Vadleány lay before him, wounded, maybe fatally, by the man's arrow.

No description given by unlucky witnesses to her horrible acts could prepare Etil for the vision of her. Even in her weakened state, Vadleány was beautiful, even more stunning than a glass of whiskey had once been to him. Her ageless, porcelain skin, a milky contrast to the dark browns of the dirt and bark around her. Etil found himself suddenly filled with worry for the woman. Was she warm enough? Would she like his coat? Maybe his shoes? The frigid winter, his own life, were no longer concerns. Would she survive?

Her eyes flickered open with an energy that said she was terrified to have let her guard down for so long. A low growl rattled in her throat. Still, she held her arms out, but her hair reached him first. The long, golden brown strands crawled across his skin, carressing and inspecting his shape. A wisp found the callouses of his working hands, tracing circles around the rough mounds.

He pulled the black, crow-feather coat from his shoulders and extended it to her. She shied away at first, unfamiliar with the gesture of offering, and winced in pain with the movement. She pet the coat, drawn in by the sheen and softness of the feathers. Her fingers followed the vanes knowingly, as though she was an old friend to each crow from which they had fallen. A length of her hair wrapped around his wrist and pulled him close to her, bringing his hand near the arrow in her side.

He nodded. "I will help you, but not here." The other villagers could not be allowed to see her. They would kill the beautiful creature on the spot. Not once did the thought cross his mind that he should do that wicked deed. He didn't want to carry her scalp into the village in triumph; to be a hero to not only his people, but the entire countryside. Maybe that's why she didn't kill him. Somehow she knew the goodness of his nature. My customers will have to wait, he told himself. She needs me. Etil wrapped her in his coat and she disappeared in its bulky warmth. He turned around and headed back.

The woods held her in; a natural barrier, a comfort zone, and all she knew. He crossed the threshold between the wild and the civilized, clutching the murderous woman like a bride brought home for the first time. If the others found out he'd brought her into the village, he'd be killed alongside her.

When he was young, he'd tended to the leg of his dog who'd stepped in a hunter's trap. It was rudimentary wound treatment and he used the same techniques to care for her now. After some pressure, the arrow came out silently and clean. He placed it on the mantel and returned to her side. He could hear the rest of the village, going about their lives as evening approached. Sitting down to warm meals, earthen platters thudding softly on wood tables, light laughter finding timid paths out of the darkness. How those noises would change if they knew what beast lay so near them.

The wild woman curled up in front of the fire he'd built for her, like a cat finding the best spot and staking claim. The flames jumped up and retreated, and just above their crackling he could hear another noise. Vadleány was asleep, making a sound that also reminded him of a feline; a husky purr. The soft display should have calmed him, her hair glowing in the firelight and her wounded body finally at ease, but the noise was pure animal. A deep motor drove this woman, one he already knew the dangers of.

The fire warmed the room and sent him off to sleep. In his dreams, the crackling of the fire warped into bones breaking and the warmth of the room became oppressive. When he woke, a brighter light filled the cabin, too much light. The sun too high in the sky. He normally woke with the rooster, but it had not crowed it's throaty call that morning. The room was cold, the fire having died sometime in the night, not even a wisp of smoke coiled up from the black ash. He hung his legs over the edge of the bed and relished the temporary confusion of waking, until his feet brushed against something on the floor. Soft feathers. Fearing looking at it, and confirming what he already knew to be true, he played his toes across the abandoned coat and took in each corner of the room. He was alone. The arrow, blood dried on it's head, lay broken in two where she laid the night before. Where was Vadleány?

It was then he noticed the stillness of the village around him. Absent was the laughter of children, the snorting of hogs, the chatter of the chickens and of the women as they praised market goods for their quality, the boisterous ramblings of the men performing the hard work of never ending repairs.

Etil dressed and donned his coat. He checked on his neighbor Ivan, a bedridden elder, first. The door was ajar, but that wasn't too uncommon, as Ivan had many daily visitors. A familiar pair of shoes sat just inside. Etil's boots met a creaky floorboard, sending a screech through the small home. It was as good as a knock to announce his presence and he waited for Ivan to call out, but no greeting met his ears.

In the bedroom, Etil found Ivan. Pieces of the infirm man dotted the bedding and floor like scrap thrown to the hogs. Etil cried out at his own foolishness as he examined the bones and flesh for the teeth marks he knew he'd find.

Home after home presented a similar scene. Blood-smeared walls, struggles for survival. No life left, only limbs. She'd eaten them all, buffet style, helping herself to all the servings she could manage.

A bellowing moan, like an explosion before a great wind, a shock wave, came charging toward him from the center of the village. The buildings creaked in weakening defiance of the gale. Etil pushed his feet into the muddy ground and walked into the invisible wall. Then, a sound unlike anything he'd ever heard surrounded him. Every leaf left on every tree in the entire wood, even the leaves already fallen to the ground, rustled and trembled and vibrated with life amid the breeze.

"Vadleány!" He called out to her, or he thought he did, but his voice was lost in the cacophony. He fought his way toward the source of the wind, like a salmon swimming upstream to spawn, determined against a powerful current.

In the center of the square, Vadleány lay naked and asleep, her belly taut and distended. The dried blood of the village matted her hair and held pieces of flesh and flecks of dirt to her skin. That he hadn't awoken to any screaming during the night was testament to her swiftness. Etil sat beside her, using her giant belly as a windbreak, and cried. A death a month, he could live with that. The village somehow found a way to live with it. But the entire town dead in one night because of him?

She'd found a way into his heart and then devoured all he knew and loved. There was no place for him in the village anymore. It was a graveyard. Each rooftop a pointed tombstone, each frozen footprint a trailing echo of a life stopped in its tracks.

He collected the shoes of the dead and placed them in a circle around the sleeping woman, hoping to appeal, upon her waking, to whatever conscience she might have. His tools fit in a small bag on his back. For once, and even in his sorrow, he enjoyed the journey on the path through the woods. The leaves danced and sang a comforting tune as he walked. He was not in danger. Not yet. The monster was still asleep.

WHEN YOU FIND OUT WHAT THEY'RE MADE OF

I set a pile of books down on the scuffed wood counter and focused my attention on a man walking through the door. "I know him from somewhere."

"Yeah, from here. He comes in all the time." Keith appeared behind me, stealth as ever in his Toms. I admit I jumped.

"But I know him from, like, somewhere other than here." He could have been my cashier at the grocery store or the gas station attendant at the place on the corner. The more I looked at him, the more I searched for that synapse of memory and meaning, the less familiar he became. I watched him too long and he became as foreign as a word writ or spoken too many times.

"Where else is there?" Keith chuckled and I joined him. Jokes were good, but bookstore jokes were the best. And it was true. Where else was there, really? The bookstore became your world if you haunted the aisles long enough. Keith had two decades at least. He wore the book smell like cologne, waxed poetically about the history of publishing, and even had his own work-in-progress that would hopefully grace the shelves one day. I was much less impressive, having spent most of the ten years prior to that writing dinner orders on a notepad, reading maybe five books tops that entire time, and I still hadn't selected a cologne.

Also, I'm not exactly known for my memory. That mental deficiency and my sorry excuse for a reading list meant I wouldn't be the best at recalling names and recommending new reads, but the Barely Bent Pages Bookstore still seemed like a good fit for me when I applied. I'd always wanted books to play more of a role in my life, and due to a layoff, a divorce and a general upending of my entire life, I'd needed a new job. Bad.

My penchant for button downs and cardigans and my need for glasses presented me as the quintessential bookseller. My constantly tired look could read as late nights spent with George R.R. Martin or Anne Rice, a booklamp snaking over my shoulder and a content cat between my legs. I fell quickly into the comfortable groove of each day, helping customers find what they were looking for; triumphant when I could locate the book in its right location in an obscure subsection of the store. Their happiness was mine and our shared interest in the written word was an instant icebreaker, even if I didn't offer much to the conversation in the beginning. The papercuts on my fingers and the book dust in my lungs became invisible badges of honor. I even began to impress myself by recalling author names or book covers when a customer mentioned a title. My dreams filled with faraway places and people's battling impressive, scale-covered villains; things my usually simple mind would never have created before.

I wouldn't say that my memory was improving. The customers continued nameless. They were scents you know you've smelt before, but you can't say when or where. And then the fear filled me that maybe they'd remember my name and I'd hate my shitty memory even more. They had help though, for my name was emblazoned on a small, printed label stuck to a plastic tag that dangled around my neck. "Scott," it announced. This barely helpful man scurrying around in front of you is know as "Scott." "Scott" is to blame.

Part to make time pass and part to aid in improving my memory, a few coworkers and I created a game. This exercise sorted and filed the customers into tidy classifications, just like the books. And indeed, the bookstore was a microcosm of humanity, with representations from all age, income, race, religious, and other brackets. The name of the game was "The Regulars." These people, the ones who visited once a week at minimum, they could be separated into groups within the Regulars general category. The next defining tier was composed of two types of Regulars: those who bought books (The Purchasers), and those who never bought anything. Not. One. Thing. They were called The Predators, mostly-and for no reason-as a nod to the films.

The Purchasers, the regular regulars, were the morning diehards in for the newest hardcover bestseller from the preternaturally prolific author category that included Patterson, Coben, Evanovich, etc… these customers would get a coffee too and maybe a paper.

They'd have original membership cards so tattered they look picked from garbage cans, run through the wash a few times, or scarred for life on a battlefield. These regulars grew up in a time before physical books went out of style and when built in bookcases came standard in homes. They were the true readers, the ones for which stories are written, the devourers of words. I considered them on par with wine snobs, reading the back covers of books like samples of vino, tasting the finish, chewing the words, selecting their next indulgence.

This group of regulars could be further subdivided into a vast number of categories including: The Veterans: a group of surly, decorated men whose stories captivate and leave you with more information than they are buying (but they are always good for a war or current events novel), The Widowers: a sad but lovely group purchasing their placeholder companions while chatting about what their beloved departed enjoyed reading, The Cat Ladies: who love only felines more than books (books about cats were a bonus, as were quilting magazines), The Stay-at-Home-Moms: using the store as a daycare and tornado alley for their little ones (but those tornadoes loved books and those moms loved coffee), The Budding Entrepreneurs, these men and women dressed smart and always knew about the newest business and motivation books on the market, The Graphic Novel Readers and The Manga Readers, collectors and consumers alike...

My favorite of The Purchasers were The Dreamers. These are the believers in things beyond aliens and Bigfoot. We're talking lizard people, conspiracy theories on conspiracy theories, and diet cookbooks that allowed you to eat as much of whatever you wanted and you'd still lose weight. Everything short of tin hats worn into store. Most of the books they'd want weren't even available on a shelf, at least not on this plane of existence. And when we offered to order them a copy of the small press or self published book, they'd refuse to give any personal info because the government was watching them. They never had emails because someone, somewhere wanted to peer into their dirty apartment through the webcam. They'd end up buying something on crystals or astrology and go back out under the chemtrailed sky of the big, bad world.

The list really does go on and on and each of these types of people certainly held their spot in what made the bookstore an amazing place. A type of heaven where everyone has a book recommendation; where you knew you were mostly among friends.

Though you shouldn't judge a book by it's cover, Keith and I had no issue with declaring what segment of the customer base anyone fell into. As soon as we saw them, we'd whisper our taxonomic ranks to each other. "Regular, Purchaser, Budding Entrepreneur."

"Nah," Keith would say, "Regular, Purchaser, Manga Reader. He's dressed up because he had a job interview."

When the customer approached the desk to ask for help finding a book, we'd wait eagerly for the name drop, be it author or title. We'd both type as fast as we could on our terminals, warring men commanding technology, hoping to sink the other's battleship first.

"I'd be happy to take you to the *Business* section, sir!" I'd declare with more enthusiasm than the situation warranted and making serious eye contact with Keith the entire time.

It was a great time, all told, but one can't have this glorious heaven without a little hell. And hell was the second category of The Regulars: the ones who came in all the time and never bought a thing. I dubbed them The Abnormal Regulars. This group also had subdivisions: The Thieves (speaks for itself, and yes, people steal a lot from bookstores), The Homeless (looking for warmth and a cheap cup of coffee), The Lost (they need to use a phone, or a bathroom, or the Wi-Fi, or all of your time), The Students (who occasionally purchased an item or a drink, but mostly wanted our WI-FI, our outlets, and our cafe tabletops to study on), The Meeting Attendees (they said "pick a central place where we can chat", the boss said "let's go to the bookstore cafe." They both ate beforehand and are only there to propose a project, close a deal, or collect a check), The Lonelies (who need a friend and you are that friend) etc...

Being the competitive sort, I was always on the lookout for new behaviors to further define the filing system. One day, after greeting several customers and being completely ignored by all of them, I stumbled upon an entirely new breed. Or maybe they weren't a new type of Abnormal Regular, just one I hadn't noticed until then.

Usually, if you roll up one leg of your pants, you're riding a bike, not stepping off a city bus. The man in half-exposed question also wore a grey tweed jacket over a bright orange, knit sweater. I expected dress shoes. His toes wiggled off the ends of too-small flip-flops.

"Hi there! What can I help you find today?" I smeared a smile on my face and raised my voice more octaves than was normally humanly possible, the very definition of customer service.

He hurried by me in a weaving path to Fiction. He was out of sorts, distracted by his own focus. He could have been drunk. I followed, as I was trained to do when things seemed out of whack. When I caught up to him, he was a bee among flowers, hovering around a few books as though he were searching for a particular nectar. Then, just as I summoned another generic greeting from my work brain, the man found what he was looking for. He pulled the book out gently from its place, coaxing it with a single finger. I couldn't read the title from where I stood, even as he faced the book out. When it rested on the books behind it, he held up a hand, palm out. It was a gesture reminding me of a crosswalk guard signaling pedestrians to stop. Something blue and quick, a light, shot from the cover of the book into his hand. He stood straighter and replaced the book in its home. Speedwalking and confusion returned me quickly to Keith before the man noticed I was watching him.

"Keith, I'm losing my mind."

"Explain." His response was usual. We often

lost our minds at the bookstore. More information was needed.

"Regular, Predator, Blue Light Out of Hand Shit!" He could sort out what I meant from the Kingdom, Phylum, and Class I'd provided. Well, assuming he knew what the hell was going on.

He smiled, looked down at the schedule and back up at me, and picked up his phone to call another bookseller over to cover the customer service desk.

In the break room, I sat and stared at my palms. Keith paced beyond the lunch table between us. "He's special."

"This is much more than special, man."

"Even though you see him, he doesn't exist in the same world we do."

"What does that even mean? What kind of an Abnormal Regular is he?"

"They have no control over their destiny."

"You're being too literary. I still don't get it."

"You really haven't sorted it out? The book he sought, it's his book."

"Authors aren't magical. I mean, they have a way with words. They create entire worlds. But they don't exchange power with paper."

"He isn't the author of the book, Steve. That man is a character from it."

My feet traveled a similarly curving and frantic

path to the same book the man had touched. It looked normal on the shelf, with no standout design or marker. On the cover, a man in a tweed jacket on top of an orange, knit sweater sat at the edge of a dock. A pair of sandals were placed neatly next to him. One of his legs was folded in, half indian-style. The other was dangling in some water below the dock. He had smartly rolled his pant leg up to keep it from getting wet. I dropped the book on the floor. It had to be a joke.

Keith, who had found me mouth agape and in shock, bent down and picked up the book. "It isn't exactly something we can disclose on the website, or at the job interview, ya know? I wanted to tell you sooner."

My mind was spinning, digging through months of customers, searching for anyone else who might fit into the Character category. "What happens when we don't have their book?"

He slid the book back into the hole it left on the shelf. "They look somewhere else."

"And what happens when no one carries their book anymore?"

"I don't want to talk about it." He moved to leave the aisle, but I grabbed his arm.

I plucked the man's book from the shelf again. "This guy is lucky, but the other ones aren't. I need to help them."

"You can't."

"Why shouldn't we help them, Keith?"

"None of this 'we' stuff. It's an unwritten rule. We do not interfere. We can't carry all the books. Nothing lives forever, Steven. Just forget about it okay. They don't buy anything anyway."

He abandoned me in the aisle, surrounded by the rotating tombstones of protagonists and antagonists. Both they and I on borrowed time.

□

My heart was heavy as I stood by and watched the Regular, Predator, Characters lose meaning. They'd come in asking for obscure volumes, which of course we wouldn't carry. The looks on their faces were akin to those of children who had lost a parent. Hopeless. It pained me, how limited the shelf space was, how that kept us from stocking anything but the newest, most sought after books. One of the dusty used book shops might have their story, but those shops were disappearing just as the characters were. Knowledge most certainly has an expiration date.

These ghosts of the literary era, these walking, dying languages, they'd wander the earth. Maybe muster their last strength to break into a warehouse. Orphans once brought to life by love, but fast becoming obsolete to technology, would chuck rocks through windows to dig through boxes for their words. Caught, arrested. Held for too long due to lack of identification. Fading faster under the unforgiving fluorescents.

Booked. Broken.

Bookless.

ABOUT THE AUTHOR

 Michelle von Eschen is a horror enthusiast from Seattle, WA. When she is not writing, she enjoys hiking and camping, playing guitar, lifting weights, dressing up in "full gore" to attend zombie-related events, web design and gaming. Her writing portfolio also includes the novel When the Dead, the novel The Spread: A Zombie Short Story Collection, a writing collection titled Last Night While You Were Sleeping, and the novella: Mistakes I Made During the Zombie Apocalypse. Several of her short stories can be found in other books including Roms, Bombs, and Zoms from Evil Girlfriend Media, GIVE: An Anthology of Anatomical Entries from WtD Books, and A Very Zombie Christmas from ATZ Publications.

After many adventures and mistakes, she currently lives in Mill Creek, WA with her twin sister, two attack cats, and a mending heart.

ABOUT WHEN THE DEAD BOOKS

When the Dead Books is a small book company run by owner and author Michelle von Eschen. We bring horror, sci-fi, and fantasy fiction from indie writers to you. Check out our complete catalog at whenthedead.com.

WHEN THE DEAD BOOKS

[HORROR AND APOCALYPTIC FICTION]

When the Dead

The Spread: A Zombie Short Story Collection

Last Night While You Were Sleeping

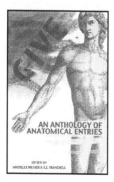

Give: An Anthology of Anatomical Entries

Mistakes I Made During the Zombie Apocalypse

www.whenthedead.com   facebook.com/whenthedead

Made in the USA
Lexington, KY
14 April 2017